THE
SENTIENT
SPACE

THE
SENTIENT
SPACE

IS THERE ANYONE OUT THERE?

Edited by Devora Gray

Stories By:

K. P. Kyle | Logan Mroczkowski | Fidel E. Arévalo León |
McKay Wadsworth | Rick Cooley |
Jay Mendell | S.L. Field | Mohammad Khan |
Zachary Sherman | Edward Swing |
Judy Backhouse | Jim Kent

4 Horsemen
Publications, Inc.

4 Horsemen Publications, Inc.
1497 Main St. Suite 169
Dunedin, FL 34698
4horsemenpublications.com
info@4horsemenpublications.com

Cover by Valerie Willis
Typeset by S. Wilder
Edited by Devora Gray

Library of Congress Control Number: 2022942652

Print ISBN: 979-8-8232-0005-9
Ebook ISBN: 979-8-8232-0004-2

Dedication

For those who believe we are meant to boldly go
where no one has gone before.

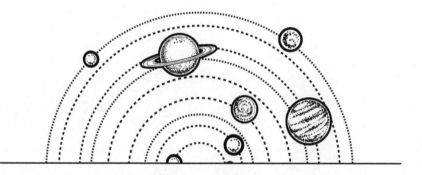

Acknowledgments

M any thanks to OG writing buddies Len M. Ruth and Brandon Mead. Whenever I'm stuck on a tricky phrase or historical space reference, they have my back. Jenifer Paquette gets all the virtual high-fives for leadership and boss editing chops. Finally, much gratitude to my dad for running *Star Trek* episodes on the daily during my childhood. We continue to look up and be amazed.

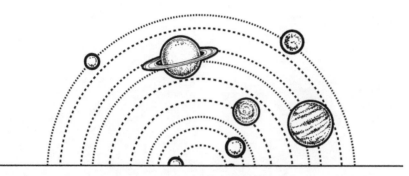

Table of Contents

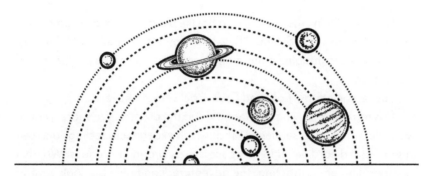

Introduction

Hello sentient friends! Thank you for joining me on an adventure into the unknown. As the editor of this collection, I'd love to share a slice of the anthology's discovery process.

There is something thrilling—and terrifying—about sitting down with a fresh stack of space stories. What will I find? The universe is vast, after all, and imagination is the ticket to new worlds, species, dreams, and nightmares.

At least I've been prepped by a childhood filled with planetariums, *Star Trek*, and Ray Bradbury.

The excitement drives the ship, and I read late into the night. At the core of my delighted angst, I hope for and find tales of intergalactic poetry in "The Ending" and brace myself through the body horror of "The Last Echo."

There's a story about a lost traveler finding a dying planet, "Utsuhi." A story about a 40-year-old woman who gets to be in her 17-year-old body, thanks to reverse space travel in "Real Time: A Story of a Thousand Year War."

Reading "Co-Creation," it's easy to fall in love with the macro wisdom of a planet interviewed by an AI-humanoid-hybrid. Reading "Hidden," I fear mind control from a micro sentience trapped on Earth.

I'm dying of thirst in "Forgotten Oasis," dying for oxygen in "A Wider Picture of the Universe," and dying to check the color of my blood after reading "In the Image of the Gods."

THE SENTIENT SPACE: IS THERE ANYONE OUT THERE?

Just when I think the universe is a hostile place for a fragile human, stories like "Any Port in a Storm," "Revelation on Hellscape," and "The Last Story" ask me to imagine a more diverse universe from the perspective of abundance.

Space, the eternal Lost and Found, delivers all the feels.

This makes sense when contemplating the prompt. We share a collective understanding of sentience—that which experiences feelings and sensations—but a hard definition of *space* is fuzzy around the edges. Whether it's expanding or contracting, the adventurer can't help but look beyond a limited horizon.

Luckily, science fiction allows sentience to trade places with sapience, or transcendent wisdom of an ultimate reality (think heaven or hell). Intuitive consciousness isn't just for the lovers of *Star Wars*, *Aliens*, and *The X-Files*. It's for anyone who has asked, "What am I feeling? What is real? How do I know I exist?"

Such exciting and terrifying concepts!

In these concepts, self-awareness is the destination. We want knowledge that feels safe and reassuring, but we're driven off-course by the fear of something superior and malignant who might deem humans obsolete. With the advent of AI and the James Webb telescope, a sure thing isn't forthcoming. A writer knows this and uses it to their advantage.

I can't say any one of these stories answer our quintessential questions, but after visiting twelve universes, the theme of the collection was revealed over a long weekend.

Sentient Space is about hope and horror. You'll find these emotions, along with humor, desperation, grief, and salvation in the following pages.

From a lover of darkness and delight to a reader of the same slant, welcome to the unknown.

Devora Gray
August 20, 2022

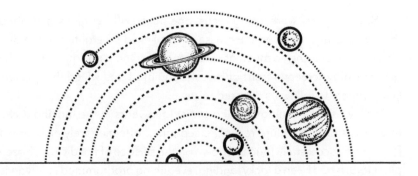

Hidden

by K. P. Kyle

Pluto.

A tiny planet—not even a planet, a tiny planetoid—whipping through the distant cold, its orbit so incomprehensibly large that by the time humanity got around to discovering and reaching out to it, it had not completed two revolutions. Icy, remote, barely brushing past the sun's outstretched fingertips, as a planet (planetoid) it held little promise of being anything other than an oversized asteroid.

Pluto paled in comparison to Europa or Enceladus or any of the other gas-giant moons with documented oceans, or the seductive Proxima B, the exoplanet beckoning from Alpha Centauri's binary star system. Any of those had the basic ingredients needed for the development of life as we knew it: the right combination of atomic elements, the right range of temperatures, water. What did Pluto have? A feather-touch of gravity, eternal darkness, and eternal cold.

Still, we've never been able to resist the allure of the unknown and never turned away from the unexplored. Just human nature, we reached out to it.

Bouvier's eyes were losing focus. She pulled off her glasses, rubbed them vigorously, replaced the glasses and blinked several times. It didn't alleviate the blurring so much as smear the blur. Too long squinting at the blank display screen in front of her, she squinted and willed the capsule *Pomegranate* to follow its directed route.

This was the culmination of a project ten years in the making. Over three years ago, the Pluto rover "Persephone," affectionately nicknamed Perse, had successfully touched down on the surface of the distant, frozen planetoid. It had been a tricky landing, everything programmed in advance with no possibility of real-time corrections, given the four-and-a-half hours it would take for radio signals to travel from Earth to Pluto and vice versa. They'd had to sit, white-knuckled in the command center, waiting to see if things had gone well or if Perse had been damaged or destroyed. An exquisite, dreadful sort of predetermination. Compared to that, tracking the capsule landing was a piece of cake.

The capsule. *Pomegranate*. Containing the secrets of the underworld. Bouvier wasn't entirely convinced the mythological allegory worked, but she had not studied Classical Western History and did not particularly care. One of their summer interns, an undergrad from the University of Chicago whose name she had forgotten, suggested the name. Something about pomegranate seeds being the link between the worlds of the living and the dead. Liberal arts kids, what can you do.

After the nail-biting but successful landing, Perse spent several months drilling core samples for examination over the surface of Pluto. The original plan had been to equip Perse as a roving space-laboratory, like the old Mars rovers of history, but Pluto's insubstantial gravity, near-lack of atmosphere, and extreme cold limited Perse's lab options. To compensate, Perse collected the samples, packed them neatly into the small *Pomegranate* capsule, and launched *Pomegranate* back to Earth.

That had been eighteen months ago. A long, lonely trek home for Perse's little seed. But against all odds—not really, Bouvier had worked hard to ensure the success of this mission, but it made for a better story—*Pomegranate* had made it home.

In the end, Bouvier had to trust it would do what it was supposed to do and the years of engineering and design would pay off. It would follow its directed route. It would. It had to.

Behind her, Samford's voice, calm and steady, belying the stress underneath. "*Pomegranate* detected, approximately forty-nine kilometers elevation, current speed 394 meters-per-second." A pause, an update. "367 meters-per-second. Deceleration slightly faster than expected, but still within parameters." None of the remaining team members in the room spoke; every one of them intent on the capsule's progress, silently hoping, silently praying.

A fuzzy dot appeared in the upper left quadrant of the otherwise black screen. Bouvier tapped at the keyboard, and the dot obligingly moved to the center of the screen but remained fuzzy. She didn't need to see it clearly—they'd received images from orbiting telescopes stationed along the capsule's long journey as it passed Jupiter's orbit, later Mars, and finally the Moon. They'd shown the capsule visibly intact, undamaged, but it would be good to see it from an Earth-based telescope.

"250 meters-per-second. Expected touchdown—uh—looks like it'll be between eight and fifteen kilometers off the coast."

Bouvier glanced back at Samford. "Our coast, correct? Just to confirm." She half smiled, half joking. Half. She didn't have cause to worry, or so she told herself. Things were going well on the capsule front.

"100 meters-per-second. Approximately twenty-two kilometers elevation. Capsule exterior temperature holding steady," Samford said, a trace of tension creeping into her voice. On the screen, the image of the capsule slowly enlarged, clarified, and sharpened. "Splashdown predicted in six minutes." The background noise in the room vanished: everyone appeared to have stopped breathing, Bouvier included, and the only sound left was the humming of the equipment, the steady beeping of the radar tracking, and the whooshing from the air-conditioning vents.

Bouvier rubbed her palms, suddenly and inexplicably icy, against the front of her thighs. Unclenched her jaw, almost immediately reclenched.

"Five minutes. Eighty-seven meters-per-second. Parachutes deployed."

Four minutes. Three. Two. The image on the screen was clear. *Pomegranate* hurtled through the lower atmosphere, dragging its chutes behind. Too fast? Too slow? Bouvier leaned closer to the screen, trying to see if there was any damage visible. Even if there wasn't, would there be, once it hit the water? Would it float, remain watertight? They had run hundreds of computer simulations of this moment, accounted for every eventuality, and objectively she was confident, assured everything would go according to plan. But computer simulations were just fancy, expensive video games, and this moment was the only moment that mattered.

Her pulse thrummed in her ear, loud, drowning out everything, even Samford's steady final countdown. "Ten seconds out. Five. Four. Three. Two..."

Pomegranate hit the water, vanished into the churning waves, and for a horrifying moment Bouvier thought it was gone—then it bobbed up, nestled in the cords and fabric of its three chutes. The sun shone off the bright red, stylized split-fruit design. Dimly, Bouvier was aware of Samford's announcement— "Splashdown successful!"—as the room erupted in cheers and whoops, almost matching the dizzying buzz of triumph in her head.

Pomegranate, up close, was bigger than Bouvier remembered. It had been nearly six years since she'd stood in the same room. Somehow, in her mind it had shrunk. Compared to the rest of the mission's equipment—the interplanetary shuttle, the massive fuel tanks needed to launch the shuttle out of Earth's atmosphere, Perse the rover was designed to be comically massive to counter Pluto's likewise-comically light gravity, lest it encounter a slight breeze and drift off course. This made it toy-sized, a mere five meters in length, cylindrical, with a two-meter diameter. Without the other equipment, isolated within the sterilized and quarantined "Clean Room" in the Extraterrestrial Recovery and Evaluation wing of NASA's Eastern Florida campus, it seemed huge, fantastic, almost unreal.

Bouvier stepped closer, laying a gloved hand against the silica-tiled exterior. During its long trek from the edge of the solar system, it had picked up a few scuffs and scratches, even a couple of alarming dents over the nose. Overall, it seemed to be in exceptionally good condition. Better than Bouvier had dared to hope, given what happened with Perse.

A short time after *Pomegranate*'s launch from Pluto, Perse had abruptly developed issues with navigation and orientation, driving itself into obstacles and finally tumbling into a crevasse to land on its side. This was weird, because it was specifically designed not to tumble into crevasses, and also designed to right itself in the event that it should fall and land on its side.

There was a debate at Mission Control as to whether the malfunction had been triggered by the recent launch of the capsule, or if it was an independent event—in which case they had gotten lucky the capsule launched before Perse's catastrophe. Regardless, Bouvier's team spent several futile months trying to coax Perse back into a functional state. They'd ultimately settled for collecting what data they could from Perse's static position, but even that became progressively challenging with inexplicable blackouts that would last from seconds to hours. Commands and queries sent from Mission Control were ignored, bouncing back nine hours later with the equivalent of an interplanetary error message.

Then about a year ago, Perse had stopped transmitting entirely. That was also weird. Perse's batteries were designed to continue functioning for an additional four Earth years, and there was no explanation for why they drained so rapidly. One of the lower-level engineers on the project, a grad student named Gardner, went so far as to suggest an unidentified characteristic of Pluto had actively sabotaged the rover, a notion which was too vague and absurd for Bouvier to take seriously.

Behind her, the airlock-sealed door opened with a hiss and whir, and the grad student in question stepped through to stand beside her. She glanced in his direction, though the hood and face-shield of her protective suit blocked most of her view: while in the clean room, all personnel were obligated to wear full protective suits with self-contained breathing units to avoid any possible contamination of the Plutonian samples, rather than the other way around. Preliminary analysis from Perse, before Perse's demise, had indicated no particular danger from the samples—no radioactive elements, no toxic or corrosive gases, nothing that needed anything more elaborate than a pair of safety goggles and maybe a high-filtration face mask—but they had to ensure any data collected from the samples would be accurate. If they were to detect traces of viral particles scattered over the surface of a Plutonian rock, they'd need to be damn sure that it wasn't because some idiot sneezed on it.

Bouvier removed her hand from the capsule, self-conscious, not wanting to appear melodramatic or unprofessional, though Gardner of all people was hardly one to judge. Even through the suit, she could hear his breath catch.

"It's incredible," he murmured, his voice slightly distorted by the layers of protective nylon and plastic but somehow brimming with childlike wonder. "Did you ever think we'd do it? Actually, touch a part of Pluto?"

Bouvier suppressed a sigh, faintly amused. "We won't be touching it, technically. Don't get too excited."

She turned to face the airlock entrance where the team geologists Tran and Herrera emerged, carrying the remaining equipment for first-pass sample analysis. They'd be starting with basic microscopic inspection, thermal analysis and mineral evaluation, and eventually move on to scanning electron microscopy, X-ray diffraction and gas chromatography. Perse had already given them an idea of what to expect, and they'd outfitted the lab, but Bouvier had to admit it felt different physically working with samples in real time as opposed to transmissions across millions of miles of empty space. Gardner was right, it was incredible. It was real, somehow, whereas Perse's transmissions had been almost detached, like the difference between witnessing an eclipse and seeing one on television.

"Ready?" Herrera asked, hand poised by *Pomegranate*'s hatch, and Bouvier nodded. Herrera fired up a cordless drill and began the elaborate process of accessing the interior compartment where the samples had been packed securely in place. There were seven of them, each measuring five kilograms, in individual discs resembling old film reels buried in the center of the capsule's body. Herrera had to jiggle the first disc to dislodge it. Flakes of asbestos drifted to the ground around her. She pulled it free, set it on the nearest lab station, and flipped the latches on its side.

They crowded around the table, Tran standing on a stepstool to see clearly, as Herrera removed the lid and revealed the fragment of Pluto inside.

There was a soft *whuff* as the lid came off, and for an instant, Bouvier thought she saw something mist-like, aerosolized. Gone before she'd registered it, most likely a trick of the light, she automatically reached to adjust her glasses and peering intensely through the plastic face-shield at the extraplanetary object.

The Plutonian rock was reddish-brown, mica-like flecks giving it a subtle sparkle. It was larger and more solid than Bouvier expected, resembling granite or basalt, something that might have come from a quarry in New Hampshire. Almost ordinary, but with a black vein of something webbed across the surface. A crack, filled by some other substance. Possibly artefactual, caused by the drilling process, the journey across the solar system, or the stronger gravity of Earth, may have altered the physical structure and fractured what would have been otherwise intact.

On the other side of the table, Tran took a glass rod and tapped the edge of the rock experimentally. The rock did not visibly react. She switched out the glass rod for a rock hammer, chiseled off a fragment which she delicately grasped with a pair of forceps and placed it in a Petri dish. She took the dish, along with her stepstool, to her light microscope.

Herrera returned to the capsule and removed the remaining six sample cases. Bouvier, being an astrophysicist rather than a geologist, politely stepped back to allow Herrera to work, but Gardner leaned closer to the exposed sample, muttering something under his breath.

"There's a crystalline structure," Tran said from behind her paired eyepieces. "Looks like quartz, maybe? Something silica-based, I think. Wish I could lick it." Bouvier glanced in her direction, having to rotate her entire torso to get her into view. That was probably a joke, probably, though sometimes Bouvier couldn't tell when Tran was being serious. Geologists, Tran especially, could be quirky. Tran's nose was smashed up against the plastic face-shield, which pushed the microscope incrementally away from her as she tried to focus on the image. She slid a polarizing filter into place, whistling softly through her teeth. "Cool..."

"Hey! Don't—what are you doing? Don't touch that!" Herrera snapped suddenly, and Bouvier spun back to see what had upset her. Gardner froze in place under her glare, peeking guiltily out from his hood, one hand hovering centimeters over the rock sample in the case.

"I didn't—" He jerked his hand back, catching the glove on the clasp of the case. He managed catch the case before the whole thing went flying across the room and plucked the glove free before taking a few steps backwards with his hands up. "Sorry. I didn't touch it. I just wanted to see...I got excited. Sorry."

Bouvier sighed. She liked Gardner, they all did—his enthusiasm was earnest and infectious, and he was smart, if sometimes careless. He'd begged to be here for the sample unpacking, even though it really didn't have much to do with his position on the team or his doctoral research, and she'd relented because refusing would have felt like swatting a puppy. Still, his presence was contingent on good behavior. Poking at extraterrestrial objects was tantamount to shitting on the proverbial carpet, so it looked like she'd have to swat him. "Look, Gardner, why don't you go work in your office for a while. I'll let you know if we find anything interesting."

Gardner's face fell, and Bouvier had to turn away to hide her sympathetic grimace. Tran caught her eye but said nothing, her face neutral. Bouvier got the impression she was resisting an urge to leap to Gardner's defense, something she'd done in the past. Bouvier frowned and shook her head, slightly, subtly, and to her relief, Tran looked away and said nothing.

"Okay. Sorry." Gardner shuffled toward the airlock door, shoulders slumped, posture defeated. He paused at the exit, looked back at them, at the rock sample in its case, and an odd expression crossed his face.

When he didn't move, Bouvier asked, impatient, "What is it?"

"I don't—" Behind the plastic shield, his eyebrows furrowed. His shoulders shuddered briefly, violently. "Do you hear that?"

"What?"

He shook his head like he was clearing water from his ears. "No. Nothing. Sorry again." He pulled open the interior airlock door, closed it behind him. Bouvier stared at the door for a moment, looking back to Herrera and Tran. They'd already returned to their work, focused, unaffected.

———————

"It's weird," Herrera said. "We've tried everything in our wheelhouse, and we can't characterize it. Is it possible it's a new atomic element? I don't want to get overexcited, but it wouldn't be unprecedented."

"If it is, we're gonna have to come up with a better name than SXQ4," Bouvier quipped. Neither of the geologists reacted. Not in a jocular mood, it seemed.

Herrera and Tran had been working on the Plutonian samples for over a week, and both of them were visibly exasperated. According to them, all of the samples from wildly disparate collection sites contained traces of the black substance—SXQ4—the same substance they'd noted in the cracks of the first sample. It had also been present on the surface of an ice chunk from the Sputnik Planitia (a plain on Pluto's northern hemisphere), a vein threaded through a cored sample taken from the Tombaugh Canyon, and evenly distributed through a fine sand-like substance collected from the Hyecho Palu crater. It wasn't radioactive or magnetic, appeared inert, but its composition remained a mystery.

For one thing, it wasn't black—its color changed, inconsistently and unpredictably, as did its texture and weight. Was it a single novel element? A compound containing multiple unknown elements?

On the other side of Bouvier's desk, Tran brushed a sheaf of papers from the seat onto the floor and dropped heavily into the chair. "I mean, it's bizarre. I'd have thought we'd get answers from the mass spectrometry, but the results are all over the place."

Bouvier leaned back, carefully removed her glasses. She had a rudimentary—better than rudimentary—grasp of geology and chemistry, but this was over her head, and she was having trouble following what Herrera and Tran were telling her. Her thoughts skittered around, unwilling or unable to latch onto anything, like she'd taken a sleeping pill. She stared at the computer screen, willed the diagrams and data sets to coalesce into something familiar. "Okay. Right. Is it...Could there be a contaminant? Or a machine error? Maybe you should you have the spectrometer serviced."

"It's not a contaminant," Tran said. "And it's not the machine, I've checked it. Multiple times. I know what I'm doing." She leaned forward, elbows on knees, glowering. "Every test gives me different results. There's no pattern. Nothing's repeatable."

Behind her, Herrera nodded, pulled a set of printouts from the papers she was cradling and handed them to Bouvier.

"How do you know it's all the same substance? It's from different sample collections, you said?" Bouvier glanced at the printouts, which made as much sense as the display on her computer, and dropped them onto her desk. "I mean, not to come off as patronizing, but have you considered you might be evaluating different things?"

"No! That's not the issue," Tran snapped, aggrieved. Clearly, Bouvier had come off as patronizing. "It's all the same substance. I know it."

"But how—"

"I know it!" Tran insisted. "Besides, it's not a matter of geographical variations. I get the same random results, regardless of which sample I use, even when I use the same sample. I mean, that's not physically possible. Do you know what I'm saying? It is a chemical and physical impossibility." Her voice had none of its usual bright humor. It was sharp, jagged, and flinty like she was a different person entirely.

Bouvier put her glasses back on, peering at Tran. "All right, all right. Sorry, I wasn't trying to imply...Are you feeling all right?"

Tran did not look all right. Her face, like her voice, had undergone an alarming metamorphosis. There were bruise-like circles under her eyes and deep lines etched into the corners of her mouth. She looked like she'd aged ten years in the past week.

"I'm fine. I just—It's frustrating. Sorry, I didn't mean to take your head off." She sighed, hung her head. "I'm tired. I need a break, maybe. I haven't been sleeping well, and I really want to get some answers, but I feel like I'm running up against a brick wall. Nothing makes sense. Something's missing, there's something I can't see. It's driving me crazy, and I'm taking it out on everyone else. I yelled at Gardner for being in the clean room with us. And he didn't deserve it, he wasn't doing anything wrong, but I got this feeling he shouldn't have been there." Tran heaved herself to her feet, which appeared to take far more effort than her slight form required. "I'm gonna head out for the day, I think. I'll see you tomorrow. No. I mean, Monday. No, what day is it? Thursday? Tomorrow. Sorry. Tell Gardner sorry, when you see him."

"Okay. Get some rest," Bouvier said, unsettled. Where was Gardner, anyway? She hadn't seen him today, she'd barely seen him this week. He seemed to spend most of his time in the clean room with the geologists. She'd have to have a talk with him. He had his own research to focus on and didn't need to get distracted just because he thought the extraterrestrial samples were nifty.

She sighed, shut down her computer, and went to find him.

Gardner wasn't in his office. Wasn't in the building at all, at least not anywhere Bouvier could think to check. She nearly decided he'd gone home for the day, and was sorely tempted to follow this example, but on an impulse, she walked across the quad to the clean room warehouse. There was no particular reason Gardner should be there, or anyone else, at this hour. Gardner couldn't get in without an escort, as he didn't have the required security pass.

But there he was, standing at the exterior door, hands in pockets, shoulders hunched, facing the closed door.

He looked over his shoulder as she approached. "Oh, great, Dr. Bouvier. Are you headed inside? I knocked but no one answered. Maybe they can't hear me." He smiled at her, though it seemed forced, and his eyes were bloodshot and hollow. Had he been crying? Had Tran really been that cruel to him? It seemed out of character, for both of them.

"No," Bouvier answered. "No one's there, they've finished for the day. I'm headed out. Did you need something? You seem—" She paused, not wanting to pry or insult him, and certainly not wanting to find herself in the position of playing counsellor. In her opinion, two adults ought to be able to handle their own interpersonal issues.

Gardner nodded, then stopped nodding, and a look of confusion flickered across his eyes. "I guess not. I thought maybe...No, I don't know what I thought. Just felt like I had to see it."

"See what? The capsule?"

He shook his head. "I don't know. Something in there. I'll know it when I see it." He rubbed at his ear, wincing.

Bouvier frowned at him. Maybe today was not the right time to have the *Stop spending so much time with the geologists* talk. "Tran said she was short with you today," she said instead. "Told me to apologize. If it upset you."

"Huh?" His brow furrowed in confusion. "No, I'm not—You sure you're not going inside?"

"Go home, Gardner."

———

Samford tore open her requisite five packs of sugar, dumped them into her coffee, and stirred vigorously. Bouvier watched in absent fascination, though she'd witnessed this ritual before. Five packs of sugar, pour over ice, add five single-serve creamers, taste, and then add another packet of sugar. Samford was from New England, raised on coffee that had been criminally over-sweetened and over-creamed and then iced—iced! In the frozen north! She generally showed up in the morning with an enormous plastic cup of caffeinated diabetes, finished it off by noon, then had to make do with the office pod-coffee since leaving the campus during working hours was, though not prohibited, strongly discouraged.

She sipped her finished beverage, made a face, but apparently deemed it acceptable enough for consumption. On her way to Bouvier's table, she plucked an apple from the fruit display.

"Anyway," she said, pulling up a chair and taking a bite of the apple. "No one knows what to make of it. We all want to think it's real, that Perse's coming back online is significant, but...Well, you know. I think it's conceivable her battery might have recharged. If something drained it—I mean, there had to have been something—and if that something, I don't know, disappeared or changed in some way... But she wasn't designed to work this way, so I'd be hard pressed to explain, though, back-to-the-wall, I could come up with something. The more likely possibility, it's a fluke that has nothing to do with Perse. There's been solar flare activity in the past month, and it could affect the readings we're seeing. It's hard to be objective when you want something to be true so badly. You know what I'm saying?"

"Yeah." Bouvier heard herself agree, stopped herself. What was she agreeing with? What was Samford talking about? She hadn't been listening. Something about Perse. Right, Perse had started transmitting again? They'd picked up signals but couldn't confirm it was Perse. Something about them being was wrong or altered or—"Have you, uh, checked for solar flare activity recently? That could affect the readings."

"Have I...Did you hear a word I said?" Samford's eyes narrowed. "I literally just said it could be solar flares."

Bouvier winced, forced a smile. "Sorry. I was thinking about something else." Lies—she hadn't been thinking about anything at all. The only thing in her head was static fuzz.

"Hmm. You and everyone else. Something must be going around." Samford took a pull off her coffee, wrinkled her nose.

"What do you mean?"

"You haven't noticed? People are on edge. I can't talk to Tran without getting snapped at. I've started avoiding her. And Herrera, I mean, I know they both have a lot on their plate, but that's no reason to take it out on everyone. Them and Gardner, for that matter. Something's off with him. I haven't seen him working on his research for weeks. He's going to have to get moving on his dissertation if he wants to have it ready to defend by the end of the year. He spends all his time with the geology team these days."

Something about what Samford was saying sounded familiar. Right, right. Gardner. Bouvier was supposed to talk to him about neglecting his research. She'd meant to do it last week. Had she not? Had she forgotten? Damn it.

Across the table, Samford shrugged dismissively and stirred her iced coffee with a plastic straw. "Could be they're all spending too much time with it. The capsule."

"*Pomegranate?*" An odd, undefined uneasiness washed over Bouvier, and her voice became accusatory. "What are you saying? What does the capsule have to do with anything?"

Samford recoiled, raised her hands in defense. "Hey, I'm not saying it has anything to do with anything, okay? I know it's your baby. It's my baby too, you know. But...Tran, Herrera, and Gardner are acting weird. I'm just pointing out the common denominator."

"*Pomegranate* isn't the common denominator," Bouvier said. "You spent over a week with it. You and the rest of the recovery team." Samford had personally supervised *Pomegranate*'s transport from the coast to the campus clean room and subsequent installation in the clean room, a laborious process that took ten days to complete. "And you're all fine. Right? Unless there's something you're not telling me."

"No. I'm not saying it's the capsule. Obviously, it's not the capsule. They're in isolation suits, right? I don't know, maybe that's it. Too much time in the suits or something. It's messing with their minds."

"Tran left? What do you mean, Tran left?" Bouvier couldn't have heard Herrera right, because what Herrera said made no sense. There was a faint but persistent high-pitched whining in her left ear, distracting her and confusing her. Obnoxious. She didn't usually have tinnitus.

"She called me this morning, right before I got here, said she couldn't stand being here any longer." Herrera was visibly agitated, eyes wide and anxious. "Wouldn't say anything else. She hung up and since then her phone's gone to voicemail. I can't get through. She's not answering texts, either. I'm worried that..." Her voice trailed off.

"Worried that what?"

Herrera shook her head. "She was acting strange yesterday. I should have said something, I didn't know if it was serious, if she was serious."

Bouvier's throat tightened. "What happened?"

"We were running an experiment on SXQ4. After suspending it in ether, we tried a flash vaporization analysis. It didn't work. I mean, it didn't get us any closer to an answer. We couldn't finish it, really. Tran had some sort of, I don't know, episode. When the sample was vaporized, she freaked out, started screaming, and shut the whole thing down. I thought she'd hurt herself, or her suit had been breached or something, maybe exposed her to toxic gases? I got her to decontamination, we checked everything out, but her suit was fine. Physically, she checked out, nothing was wrong. When she calmed down, she said she'd had this feeling like she'd..." Herrera stopped talking, dropped her eyes. "It didn't make any sense."

"What didn't?"

"She said she felt guilty. Guilty, like she'd done something terrible. Killed someone's dog, or committed a war crime, something unforgivable. I mean, I tried to talk her down," Herrera said, "but she was being totally irrational. Said she couldn't keep working on SXQ4, said it was a sin. I mean. A *sin*." She paused, added uncomfortably, "And what's weird is...I felt like that too. Like we were doing something wrong, or...cruel, somehow, even though that's absurd. I can't explain it."

Bouvier felt lightheaded and put her hand out to steady herself on the wall. The ringing in her ear was louder. It had spread to the right side. "Okay. I'll reach out to her, get her a welfare check, or—" Was that the right term, *welfare check*? It was taking such an effort to form thoughts. "I'll have someone go and check on her. Try not to worry."

Two weeks later, Bouvier knew it was past time to get the project running again. Unfortunately, in the wake of the events of the past few weeks, the project had ground inexorably to a halt.

Tran had died in a freak accident the morning she'd called Herrera. She'd lost control of her car, spun off of the highway, across three lanes of oncoming traffic and into a telephone pole. No alcohol or sedatives in her system, just acetaminophen and ibuprofen. Maybe asleep at the wheel, maybe swerving to avoid a deer. No one could say.

Herrera took it the hardest, which wasn't surprising, given how closely they had worked together. After the accident, Bouvier told her to take as much time as she needed, to process and adjust. Herrera had nodded, silent, numb, and left the office. She hadn't spoken to Bouvier since, hadn't returned to campus, and today, she'd sent an email submitting her resignation.

After the accident, everyone had been in shock to think about the project, and the seven extraterrestrial samples were left undisturbed in the clean room next to *Pomegranate*. Bouvier tried to occupy herself by reviewing the data Tran and Herrera had gathered, which made little sense when they'd first presented it to her, and made less sense now. She wasn't qualified to move forward with the project herself—she needed a geochemist, someone with experience studying foreign or unknown substances. She needed Herrera.

Which was why she was standing on Herrera's front porch, leaning on the doorbell.

Herrera's son, a teenager, tall and gawky, with a spray of acne across his forehead, answered the door. Bouvier had known his name at some point, but she couldn't remember. She smiled, tried to look unthreatening and friendly, and said, "Hi. Is your mom home?"

The kid's eyes narrowed almost imperceptibly, and after a half-second pause, he hollered "Mom!" over his shoulder without taking his gaze off of Bouvier.

Awkward silence. Bouvier tried a bit of small talk to break the tension. "No school today?"

"It's Saturday." He nailed the adolescent attitude of bored disdain.

Bouvier was spared further embarrassment when Herrera appeared behind her son. She tapped his shoulder and murmured, "It's okay, Rudy." Rudy gave Bouvier one last skeptical glance and left. Herrera crossed her arms, stood in the doorway, somewhat pointedly not inviting Bouvier inside.

Bouvier wasn't prepared for her appearance. She had only seen Herrera in office-casual professional attire, hair slicked against her head in a tidy, practical bun. This morning, she was wearing sweatpants and an old, oversized T-shirt, and her hair was loose and tangled. Then again, as her son had pointed out, it was Saturday morning. Plenty of people dress schlubby on a Saturday morning.

"I got your email," Bouvier said, when it became apparent that Herrera wasn't planning on speaking.

Herrera nodded, frowning.

"I understand..." Bouvier started. "I mean, we all understand what you're going through. I'm not here to convince you of anything." Lies, lies.

She was absolutely there to convince Herrera to come back to the project. If not permanently, at least during a transition process, until they could find an adequate replacement. "I'm just here to talk."

"I'm not going back there," Herrera replied, tense, guarded. "I can't. No one else should, either. That place. That...stuff. It's not right, Bouvier. It's haunted."

Whatever Bouvier was expecting Herrera to say, this wasn't it. "What?"

Herrera's eyes flicked over Bouvier's shoulder, scanned the street behind her. "You know, don't you? You must know. That's why Tran—It wasn't an accident, what happened to her." She rubbed her arms, as if cold, despite the Florida heat. "It drove her to it."

Bouvier took a few beats to collect her thoughts, trying to parse out what Herrera was telling her. Failed. "I don't know what you mean. Drove her to what?"

"It gets in your head," Herrera hissed through gritted teeth. "It messes with your mind, it scrambles your brain, don't you get it? Don't you feel it? I thought it was me, I thought I was going crazy. I was hearing things, I was seeing things that weren't there. I should have known. I should have stopped us. If I had said something, she'd still be alive. She'd still be here." Her face twisted into a mask of rage or pain, both. Tears appeared in the corners of her eyes, which she wiped away with the heel of her hand. "It's too late now, it's too late. I'm infected. Look. Look, do you see that?" She pointed with her still-wet hand, past Bouvier's head, toward the sky.

Bouvier turned and gasped.

The sky, a clear blue when Bouvier had walked up Herrera's front steps, had changed to a roiling maelstrom: whorls of dark red and greenish black bands twisting across the horizon, massive spirals curling into and around each other, the sun hidden behind massive thunderheads, flickering ominously with blue-white lightning—

"Mom," Rudy said. "Mom, come inside. It's okay."

Bouvier tore her eyes from the storm and spun back around. Herrera's mouth was pulled back in a grimace of horror, her eyes wide and terrified, but behind her Rudy had reappeared, hand on his mother's arm, wholly undisturbed by the display before them. This made no sense, unless the kid was blind, or profoundly oblivious. She turned back—

It was gone. The sky was again a brilliant azure, bright and cloudless, lit by a scorching morning sun. A couple of jays flew past, alit in the tree in

Herrera's front yard and screeched angrily at each other. Across the street, a car pulled out of a driveway and drove away. A dog on a leash stopped to sniff at grass by the sidewalk, cocked a leg, and squirted a couple of drops before moving on. Utterly banal. Utterly normal.

Bouvier felt lightheaded, dizzy.

"You saw it," Herrera murmured beside her.

Bouvier nodded, almost relieved she hadn't imagined it. "What was that?"

"Stop the project. Shut it down. Get rid of the samples, all of them. Burn them, or bury them, or shoot them off into space. They're dangerous. It's dangerous." Herrera's voice was strained, shaking. Behind her, Rudy said, "Mom, come inside. It's okay." Herrera took a step backwards into the house, and Rudy, glaring balefully at Bouvier, shut the door.

———

The coffeemaker burbled, hissed, and spat out a stream of coffee. Bouvier blew on it a couple of times, tried to sip—too hot—and considered throwing an ice cube in so she wouldn't have to wait to drink it. God, she was exhausted. She couldn't remember when she'd last slept. The last two nights she'd taken a sleeping pill and found herself lying awake, forcing her muscles to relax and her jaw to unclench. She fought a constant low-level and drug-resistant anxiety. Every time she'd start to drift away, she'd jerk back awake feeling like she'd forgotten something, something was missing, something was wrong. Nothing was, but some part of her brain remained unconvinced.

Because something *was* obviously wrong.

She hadn't spoken to Herrera since the sky event, whatever it was, last weekend. She'd sat in her car in front of Herrera's house afterwards, shaking and chill-sweating, struggling to understand what had happened. A shared delusion? Some sort of mass hysteria type thing? Psychosomatic empathetic neuro-derangement? Had she somehow been dosed with a hallucinogen, without her knowledge? She'd stared at the crystalline sky, hands death-gripping the steering wheel, waiting for the bizarre celestial tempest to reappear, but nothing. Eventually, she'd left and managed to convince herself, whatever it was, it wasn't what it seemed to be. She must have imagined it, stress or anxiety or lack of sleep making her susceptible to the power of suggestion. She'd assumed Herrera had witnessed the same thing, but even that might not be accurate. Herrera could have been referring to something else, a bird or a funny cloud.

Still, the thought of returning to that house filled her with terror.

She needed to find replacements for Herrera as well as Tran. Despite the recent setbacks, the tragedy, Herrera's compromised mental status, the project was too important to be shut down. In the meantime, maybe Gardner could pick up where Herrera and Tran had left off. He'd spent enough time with them, tagging along like a curious toddler whenever he could convince them to escort him into the clean room. She hadn't seen much of him since the accident; he'd drifted, ghostlike, through the halls and offices, withdrawn and silent. Clearly, the twin losses had been an emotional blow. He was a sensitive kid, poor thing. She hoped he'd be up to the challenge.

She found him hunched over his laptop, nearly invisible behind a mass of papers, discarded paper cups, wadded tissues and other detritus. His shoulders jerked as she entered, and he looked almost guiltily, like she'd caught him looking at porn.

What she saw shocked her. Gardner's eyes were red and sunken, his lips cracked, one nostril rimmed with crusted mucus. His hair seemed thinner, and it was definitely unwashed and greasy. There were yellowish stains down the front of his shirt, in the armpits as well, and he stank of sweat and halitosis. He pulled his face into some semblance of a smile in greeting, but dropped it a second later, like the effort was too much for him, and went back to whatever he was doing on his laptop.

"Jesus, Gardner," she said before she could stop herself. "What the hell?"

"Hi, Dr. Bouvier," he said, his voice hoarse. He coughed a couple of times, cleared his throat. "Sorry, I know, it's a mess in here."

Bouvier looked around the room. The wastepaper basket under his desk was overflowing with empty food packaging, ramen bowls, and dirty paper napkins. Several textbooks lay open on the floor, one with the page half torn out. A half-empty handle of vodka was on the windowsill. Her gaze lingered on the vodka for a moment. Gardner was not handling things well. Much worse than she'd thought. "Have you been sleeping here or something? What's going on?"

"Sleeping? No." He almost laughed, rubbed his arms. "Can't sleep. Not here, not at home, not anywhere, not ever." He seemed to be having trouble forming the words. "I think I have to finish this first. I think that's the thing. I just have to figure this out and then things will be...better."

"Finish what? What are you talking about?" Bouvier picked her way through the room and looked over his shoulder at his laptop screen. He had sixteen tabs open and scattered over the desktop, none of which, to her relief, seemed to be pornographic. They were completely random. A missing persons site, what looked like a paper on genetic disorders, a fund-raising page for a starving artist. Nothing had anything to do with his actual dissertation. Add that to the list of concerns. "Gardner, what exactly are you working on?"

"It's..." He turned to face her, his eyes clouded. "I—I lost something. No." He shook his head. "Not me. *It* lost something. It got lost."

Bouvier set the coffee down on a relatively stable-appearing spot on the desk, alarmed. She'd expected Gardner to be struggling, but this was beyond struggling. This was a crisis. She'd have to call someone, a counselor or mental health professional. "I don't know what you mean. What did you lose?"

"You don't feel it?" He seemed genuinely perplexed. "You saw it, though. You were there."

"Saw what, Gardner? You're not making any sense."

He squeezed his eyes shut, pressed his hands over his ears. Took a deep breath, and when he spoke again, his voice was less frenetic. "It wants to go home. I think. Or the planet wants it back, it's hard to tell, but either way. Sorry. Planetoid." He opened his eyes again, stared at her earnestly. "We stole it. We had no right."

"The planet wants it back?" There was a phone in the room, mounted on the wall by the door. Calls were largely limited to intra-office for security reasons, but she was pretty sure there were emergency dial-out options.

"It's not a planet. Or it's not just a planet. Planetoid. It's...it's trying to communicate with me. With us."

"You mean Pluto? That planet?" *Planetoid*.

"It's trying, and we're not listening. We're not listening. You're not listening."

"Gardner," Bouvier said slowly, carefully, reasonably. "Pluto is an inanimate object. There's no life on it. It's not—"

"No!" Gardner cut her off. "No, you can't know that. You don't know that. God. We're so...so arrogant, thinking we know what life is, what life

THE SENTIENT SPACE: IS THERE ANYONE OUT THERE?

could be, like we know anything at all—We don't!" Frantic again, border-line hysterical. "We don't know everything about *this* planet. How could we start to understand another one? That stuff Tran was working on? That...SXQ4 shit? We don't know the first thing about it, what it is, where it comes from, or even—We don't know *Pluto's* origins. We know nothing!" Spittle flecked the laptop screen, and he slammed it shut.

"Calm down," Bouvier said, though she knew the uselessness of telling someone to *calm down*. What else was she going to say? The man was raving, spouting nonsense. And hyperventilating, his breath wheezing in his throat, his face panicked. Shit, she though, he's having a heart attack or something.

She darted to the phone by the door.

"Wait—wait—don't—" Gardner protested, but his eyes rolled back, and his body crumpled to the ground, knocking over the wastepaper bin. Loose papers scattered across the floor, and Bouvier dialed for help.

Gardner wasn't dead. It was the best spin Bouvier could put on the situation. He wasn't dead, but he was carted away semi-conscious in an ambulance. He'd fought the restraints on the gurney until one of the EMTs managed to inject him with a sedative. Bouvier watched from a distance, fighting tears. "Probably a panic attack or a mental breakdown," the EMT told her as she gave them Gardner's emergency contact information. Bouvier had nodded dumbly, unable to form a coherent response.

She had to shut down the project.

Tran. Herrera. Gardner. Samford was right—There was a connection, a common denominator. But it wasn't the capsule. It was from inside the capsule, something that had been released, or unleashed, in the clean room.

SXQ4. That mysterious, unidentifiable substance that had so upset Tran, it was toxic, somehow—had to be. It must have caused a neurochemical imbalance, acted like a hallucinogen, driven them mad (for want of a better term). Had they been careless? The isolation suits should have protected them. Maybe they hadn't taken the appropriate precautions, maybe they'd assumed they were safe. There was a cc-camera in the clean room; she should go through the footage, see if there had been a breach in protocol.

What if the suits weren't protective, after all? Possibly the effects could penetrate the fabric like radiation—except it wasn't radiation— they'd checked for radiation. Then again, it wasn't so terribly long-ago humanity didn't know about radioactivity, didn't know how to protect against it. Was it so outlandish there may be something new, unidentified and dangerous, carried back to Earth on the capsule?

Tran, Herrera, and Gardner had exposed themselves to the alien samples in the clean room. Not once, but repeatedly, and for prolonged periods. That had to be why they'd been affected, them and only them. No one else was in the room, not for any significant lengths of time. Except for herself, of course, but only once, which was probably why she hadn't experienced what they had. Why she could still behave rationally.

The contaminant had been quelled while it was in the sample containers. The suits hadn't been adequate protection, but the layers of steel and ceramic and insulation were.

Now that she understood, Bouvier knew what she had to do.

———————————

Bouvier stumbled across the campus, almost in a trance. A tiny lizard darted across the sidewalk in front of her feet, vanished into grass damp from last night's auto-sprinklers. The sun beat aggressively down on her head and shoulders, and its brightness washed out her vision. The ringing in her ears made it hard to concentrate. Still, she walked. She had to get to the clean room, had to put things right.

The solution was simple, painfully simple: the samples had to be re-isolated, back in their cases, back in the belly of the capsule, until she could come up with a long-term solution. She had to neutralize the danger.

She reached the warehouse and waved her pass at the security badge reader. Distantly, she heard it beep. The door unlocked.

She'd be exposing herself to the contaminant, the toxin, whatever it was, in doing this. No way around it. But she'd already been exposed; no point in putting anyone else in danger.

This time she didn't bother with the isolation suit. It clearly didn't provide adequate protection and putting it on was a laborious two-person job. Last time Gardner had helped her, but now...What was the point? She waved her pass at the clean room airlock, and the door slid open. A moment in the airlock, then the door opposite opened, and she stepped inside.

Everything seemed normal. *Pomegranate* was in the center of the room, supported by an array of struts and girders, still gleaming, though somewhat scuffed and battered. She couldn't help feeling the old familiar swell of pride, followed by a wave of despair and guilt. She'd had such expectations for this project, so much hope. It was her baby, just like Samford had said, but it had become something ugly, something malevolent. She had to put it down, like Old Yeller. Bouvier swallowed the knot forming in her throat and willed the tears from her eyes.

The Plutonian samples lay in their seven cases on the geologists' workstation. One case was open, presumably the one Tran had been working with when she'd had her initial "freak-out" as Herrera had put it. It had been left untouched since Tran's death. The sample inside was familiar: reddish-grey stone, cracked, a glittery dusting of a black granular substance scattered over top. SXQ4. Strange, exotic. Almost beautiful.

Almost? It was beautiful. Mesmerizing. It had travelled an unimaginable distance, from a place untouched by human hands, unseen by human eyes. Bouvier had made it happen! No one had ever accomplished what she had. Regrettable consequences or no, the significance of her accomplishment couldn't be denied. She'd discovered something new, this incomprehensible substance, this cosmic mystery. Despite everything, she deserved to feel a little pride.

She leaned closer, tilted her head slightly. It seemed to have a resonance, almost ringing. Singing. Was that the tinnitus? No, the tinnitus was gone.

Bouvier found herself reaching for it. Stopped with a finger inches from the surface, fighting an overwhelming compulsion to touch the rock.

Why shouldn't she touch it? When would she have this opportunity again? Why should she deny herself this chance?

She jerked her hand back, straightened up. What was she doing? Standing here, dithering over toxic substances. Clearly, she was being affected. She picked up the lid to the sample container, locked it in place, and packed the case safely in the belly of *Pomegranate*.

Except she didn't.

The lid was still sitting on the table, untouched. The sample case lay open, the stone inside exposed, and she couldn't tear her eyes away. Hypnotized. Seduced.

It was more than just a rock, wasn't it? Something beyond a simple physical object, minerals and elements and atoms and subatomic particles that couldn't be identified but could be felt and seen. It was something... in-between.

She reached for it, again. It reached for her.

A crackling noise from the intercom speakers. Samford's voice. "Bouvier, what are you doing? Get out of there!"

Dimly, Bouvier knew something was wrong. But her thoughts were clouded, muffled. Something was crowding them out, a notion coalesced to a realization. This substance, this celestial element, this essence of a distant world: *it was sentient, it was aware.* It was trying to communicate. Like Gardner had said.

Her finger brushed the sample. Black—blue—green—black again, sandy particles stuck to her fingertip, thrilling, tingling. She'd never seen anything so wondrous, never felt such euphoria. It swept up her mind, her consciousness, swirling, roiling, tumultuous.

Samford's voice was still coming through the speakers, shouting. Samford. What did Samford know? Nothing. She wouldn't understand. She'd never understand.

Bouvier didn't understand, either; none of this made sense. She didn't care, though. She could sense the message, not in words but through some deeper connection beyond language.

It wasn't malevolent, after all. Bouvier had been wrong about that. It meant no harm. It was...sad. It was lonely. It was hurt.

How could she have failed to see this? How could she have overlooked something so clear, so simple? The guilt in her chest blossomed and constricted, pulsed. She was at fault, she was to blame. She had gone to a distant place, a place she hadn't understood, hadn't even tried to understand, and she had violated it, attacked it, stolen a piece of it and imprisoned it. She'd committed an atrocity, an unforgivable sin. It hadn't wanted to hurt Tran or Herrera or Gardner. It just wanted to be whole again. It wanted be set free, to be left alone.

This was on her. Her responsibility. She had to fix it. She had to release it.

THE SENTIENT SPACE: IS THERE ANYONE OUT THERE?

Bouvier lifted the alien rock from the sample container and cradled it in her arms. An alarm sounded, blaring, obnoxious, irrelevant, as she exited the warehouse and offered the Plutonian entity to the Florida sky.

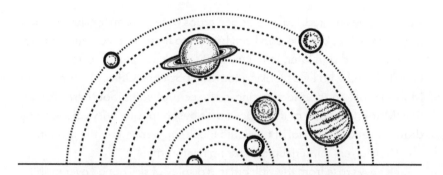

A Wider Picture of the Universe

By Logan Mroczkowski

The Magna Tree was dying. Plain and simple. We had our best people working on it, but test after test, day after day, all say the same thing: *we are dead.*

I, that "I" being one Captain Doctor Harris Richter (I never knew whether the Doctor or the Captain should come first), walked into the communal arboretum of *The Magna*, the International Biological Space Exploration Association's newest universal transport flagship. The Magna was a next generation bio-craft, running on the newest and most advanced "flora-technology," if you believe the bullshit IBSEA pedals. Bullshit that, given the current circumstances, I was having a hard time being peddled.

The Arboretum, usually abuzz with the activity of children and families gathering around the swings and slides hanging from the branches that coursed through the large domed ceiling, stood near abandoned. Scanning the room, I found the blob of scientists in white safety jumpsuits and strode toward them.

The usual verdant green shades coloring the trees of the gardens were missing, as if stolen by a thief in the night. They had adopted a sickly gray pallor and did nothing to aid the dismal atmosphere present in the ship for the last month. It made me shudder. The branches that ran throughout the ship were at their worst nearest to the trunk of the Magna Tree. The bark was split and cracked, leaving jagged crags wide enough for slow-motion fountains of black sap to drip from branch to floor like colosseums of old.

A resigned sigh later, I tried my best to pick out one specific jumpsuit. I finally found who I was looking for, Chief Science Officer Dr. Emmylou Marren. Tall, stern, and sporting an accent of some Southern disposition, Marren was one of the spacecraft's best hopes for survival. She was drawing yet another vial of the liquid black sap pooling on the ground.

"Dr. Marren," I interjected, clearing my throat.

Her eyes rose from the vial, but in a display of skill honed over months of repeating this same task, her hands continued the task of drawing sap.

"Harris. What do you need?" she said with surprising brusqueness. Upon realizing how she phrased the question, she released a deep sigh, relaxed her shoulders, and muttered, "Sorry, Captain."

"No harm done, Emmylou. We all feel that way around here. I came to ask for a status report, but I'm presuming not much has changed?"

"Not at all," she replied. "Our engine is dying, our life support is failing, and the power supply alongside it—" Her eyes focused on the portion of The Magna Tree's trunk where branches expanded outward to all sections of the ship. "The Magna Tree is dying, being poisoned, more specifically."

"Well, what about—"

Marren broke in, "Who the hell thought it was a great idea to make a spacecraft run off a single tree? Is there no fail safe? No backup generator? Nothing at all?!"

I stretched out my arm in an attempt to comfort her, but it came across as awkward and forced. I was never good at these sorts of things.

"No, Doctor Marren, there isn't a fail safe." Letting my arm hang awkwardly at my side, I hoped the gesture went unnoticed. "Far as I can tell, I've scoured every bit of the computer that isn't stuck behind IBSEA encryption, and there is nothing of use."

"Damnable corporations and their secrecy," she spat "Do they think we are going to leak their tech to the competition tens of thousands of lightyears away from Earth?"

I shrugged and shook my head.

She continued, "Listen, Harris, I've gotta get these samples back to the lab, but based on the rate of decay, we have about two weeks of oxygen left."

I nodded. The cracks splitting the branch system weaving in and out of the metallic architecture of the ship looked worse than they had a few days prior.

"Get on it, doctor. At least we have a timeline now." I hoped I sounded more determined than I felt.

Without a word, she nodded, gathered the vials of sap, and made her way to the lab.

It felt like days since I had slept, and thinking back, it may have been. Wearily entering my quarters, I tossed my uniform on the floor and kicked off my boots, making sure neither landed in an ever-growing pool of black sap. I made a mental note to call Custodial and have them send someone down. Flopping on my bunk in a most undignified manner, I reflected the room was spacious, approximately three times the size of most quarters on the ship. It was one of the big draws for me when I asked to become Captain. The irony of one who loves his space and has willingly deciding to lock himself aboard a vessel with a finite amount was not lost on me.

The decor was minimal, but the highlight of the room was the natural sprawl of branches that wove in and out of the ceiling. When I first boarded the ship, the ceiling was awash in a canopy of greenery and bioluminescent blue flowers. Now, I was left with a constant ooze of sap threatening to drip on me while sleeping. The last flower had died weeks ago. The Captain's quarters were no longer appealing.

As I sprawled on my bed, an array of images rushed through my head. Thoughts of the Magna Tree, the black ooze, even the lives of the multitude of people on board raced through my sleep-deprived mind. The clearest thought rang the loudest. *How did I get here?*

I was a respectable enough scientist and soldier back on Earth. Graduated top third of my class at New West Point. (The historical West Point was deemed no longer safe due to water intrusion). No specific honors, no commendations, but I did well enough to graduate and get free drinks in bars around town from people "thanking me for my service." I did my time in an unremarkable career piloting drones in the outer reaches of the Kuiper Belt. Deciding to pursue my doctorate in Computer science, I landed a pretty sweet gig with the US AstroNavy. However, I noticed a trend. I was never what one would call a patriot, but I certainly didn't sign up to take orders from corporations. Somehow, that's what I was doing.

Programming proprietary applications for "The US," the software was bankrolling the government.

Watching my country and more importantly my time, slowly devoured by a corporatocracy masquerading as a democracy was too much for me to handle. So, I made a bit of an ass of myself, not on purpose of course, getting drunk at some gala, and talking too much to people who I didn't know were corporate bigwigs. Boom, next thing I know, I am a pariah from the industry and can't find a job within a hundred yards of a computer.

IBSEA found me flipping burgers two years later. They asked if I wanted to join their new deep space exploration mission. The thought of working directly for a large corporation disgusted me, but IBSEA was a new kid on the block. They talked a big game about being a "unique type of corporation," whatever that meant. Either way, they suckered me in, passed me through what seemed like a very mild screening, and handed me a Captain's jacket. It seemed too convenient back on Earth, and in the deepest reaches of space, I *knew* it was too convenient. It didn't take long to piece together the majority of the crew were dissidents of our new corporate overlords. We had all been duped, and the best we could do was survive to spite them.

I finally drifted off to sleep while cursing myself for being so stupid.

The next "morning," or nearest approximation thereof, it was confirmed we had thirteen Earth days of oxygen left, and if nothing was done, the entire crew and their families would die fighting for breath. On top of that, the chemical poisoning the tree was standard glyphosate. All that remained was to find out who was doing it and why. It fell to me to deliver the news to those aboard, and I sent out a message via the comms system.

"Meeting in twenty minutes. Top Priority. Conference Hall C."

As the faces began emerging through the doorway, I pointed out the black ooze in the doorway, asking them not to slip. The crowd settled into their seats, and silence invaded the room. I rose from my seat behind the podium. They knew what this was about and hoped for good news, but the look I was trying (and failing) to hide on my face told them what needed to know.

"Thank you for coming on such short notice. I guess since we can't leave the ship, it's not like you had anywhere better to be—" I forced a weak chuckle.

No one in the room blinked.

I cleared my throat. "As of this morning, we have confirmation. The Magna Tree, our source of energy, air, and life is being poisoned. Effectively, every man, woman, and child has three hundred and twelve hours to live. We do not know who is doing this or why, but in thirteen short days, they will have killed us and themselves, no matter their purpose."

The stillness was replaced by a new silence, something deep and primordial, one heard by creatures who had just received a death sentence.

"Captain," the head of Botanicals, a woman named Dr. Walker, chimed in, "What is our next step?"

It heartened me to see this group of dissidents standing resolute in such conditions, and I knew I had to do the same.

"Botany and Biology will be working together to drum up the ingredients to counteract the glyphosate poisoning. Security, Medical, and Psychiatry, I want you to keep the peace around here. Navigation and Engineering, I want you to work together to find anything in our vicinity that is habitable in which we can possibly land. Custodial, redouble your efforts to clean up as much of this sap as humanly possible. We need to keep morale high, and I think the best way to do that is keeping this ship clean. Finally, myself and the Science team will be working on getting into the encrypted files to try and wrest control of the ship from those bastards at IBSEA. All reports are to be made daily to Dr. Marren."

A murmur of confirmation rose through the group. They must have felt better knowing they had tasks and could do their part to save us.

"One final thing, team. This is going to be a stressful time for all of us, I won't sugarcoat it. But I do NOT want you to lie to your staff and families. Report back to them immediately. Keep it plain, keep it upbeat, but most important, keep it simple. There is a real chance of panic spreading throughout the ship, especially as the days progress. We are going to need each and every one of you to keep their heads on straight."

Nods and assent once again filled the room as I dismissed the meeting. I was off, back to what would be my station for the next thirteen days. There was no way I was going to let this ship fail.

It only took three days for the first incident to occur. I had assumed it was going to happen eventually, but I didn't think it would be so soon.

Managing to break away from my position in front of the computer mainframe, I decided it was time to grab food and headed for the general mess hall. I heard a sharp gasp rise above the din of the crowded room.

The gasp was followed by desperate screams and words I couldn't make out from across the hall. By the time I made it over to the boy writhing on the floor, a crowd had already formed around him. Thinking he was choking, I made the effort to push through the crowd, and heard what he was saying.

"THE AIR IS GONE. I CAN'T BREATHE. IT'S COMING. IT'S COMING. WE'RE ALL GOING TO DIE!"

My blood ran cold. *Not here, not now, not in such a crowded place.* This was going to be very bad if we didn't handle it quickly.

I reached the boy as he was lying on the ground tearing at his throat, leaving increasingly sanguineous streaks running down his neck and staining his clothes. I motioned to two of the larger bystanders to hold his arms down and attempted to make eye contact with the boy. His eyes were frantic, darting around the room as if looking for some sort of salvation from this bout of psychosis. His breaths heaved and labored, as if he really was running out of oxygen. After a stern "HEY" from me, the boy caught my eyes and seemed to calm down the slightest bit. The mess area gathered to see the disturbance. This was an entirely too public an event. Finally, he quieted down and began muttering under his breath. I couldn't make out much from the lad's ravings, other than one word he said sprinkled throughout the gibberish.

"Dream."

I motioned for the two men to take him out of the hall and to the infirmary, away from the ever-growing crowd.

As they pushed through the door, I turned to face a crowd of hundreds of faces staring at me in terror. They expected an explanation or assurance, but I had nothing to say to them. It was as if the same phantom force driving the young child to madness had taken any semblance of logical thought I could deliver to these people. Panicking, I pushed through the crowd, muttering something about checking on the boy, and bouts of mania due to stress. My heart pounding out of my chest, I left in desperate search for anywhere to be alone to collect myself.

Several hours and one long spell of self-loathing later, a timid knock-knocking came upon the door of my quarters.

"Captain?" The twang of Dr. Marren found my ears. "You in there?"

My chest heaved in a deep sigh. I knew I couldn't ignore the knocks forever.

"Come on in, Emmylou." A crack of light from the outside hall illuminating the room. "How's the boy?" I asked meekly.

Her eyes hardened, "Not good, Cap. He's still unresponsive, mostly gibbering, but he's not screaming, so there's an upside." My shoulders sank. I didn't even know the boy's name, who his parents were or what might have accounted for this attack. I did, however, know that in the end, it was not a good sign. I had handled the situation poorly. Mechanically, I could react to a situation with the best of them, but when it came to people—I failed yet again.

Dr. Marren looked at my furrowed brow and took the time to sit down next to me on my bunk. She gently placed a hand on my back. I didn't feel better by any measurable standard, but it helped in some imperceptible way.

I wished for nothing more in that moment than to be able to do that for others.

She looked at me and said, "It's not all doom and gloom, Cap. I came to give you an update. Well, it's mostly doom and gloom, but not all."

Her wry smile heartened me ever so slightly. I nodded, and she gave me the entire report.

Her team confirmed glyphosate had been continually injected into the tree since what seemed like an inconsequential point in space. The issue being, anything that could be used to counteract the poison was expressly forbidden by IBSEA upon leaving Earth, and thus was millions of lightyears away.

It didn't take a genius to see what was happening. For some reason, be it malicious intent or pure incompetence, IBSEA was attempting to kill everyone on board. Occam's Razor told me they just wanted to fire their dissenters off into space for their own sick enjoyment, but it seemed too expensive and complex for such a simplistic answer. Regardless of IBSEA's motives, I knew getting into the ship's automated systems was our only hope of survival. There was no way I was going to let those corporate bastards kill us.

My newfound revolutionary spirit was noted by Dr. Marren, but she still felt the need to interject, "There is one more thing, Harry."

"Hmm?" I responded, my mind racing toward a solution.

"The Dream, Harry," she said. "Over the past few days, there has been a dream going around the ship."

"Around the ship?" I posited, confused by what she was trying to tell me. "Like a cold?"

"Seemingly, yes. Reports have been coming in from every deck, at all hours of the day. Everyone is having the same dream." Her eyes lowered to the ground as if ashamed to bring something so inconsequential to my attention.

Her talk of sleep suddenly reminded me of my lack thereof. I hadn't slept since the meeting with the department heads, and my body was feeling it. "Emmylou, it's just a dream. I understand it's unnerving, but it's probably from the stress." I paused, considering my next words carefully. "Do me a favor and send a ship wide notification. If you are unable to sleep, see Dr. Yang in Psychiatry. She will give you something to help you sleep. Now Emmylou, I need some sleep."

A dubious look crossed her face, but I was too tired to question it. She nodded and gave me one final pat on the back before striding to the door.

"Glad you're feeling better, Captain. There's always tomorrow to do better."

She smiled, winked, and left me in darkness. Feeling slightly better about myself and my ability to captain a ship, I hit the bed and was asleep immediately.

And then the dream began.

I was walking alone in the arboretum, the Magna Tree standing in front of me, alive and thriving. It was still growing, ever taller and lusher, until it stood cramped and crushed by the metal confines of the spacecraft.

That is, until small discrete cracks began forming in the bark of the tree. The black liquid was soon pouring out of the tree in torrent of viscous ooze, trying it's hardest to sweep me away. I held my ground, but the tide rose. Soon it was past my knees, my waist, rising to my shoulders until my head was completely covered, and I could no longer breathe. Panic set in immediately. I was lost in complete blackness and struggled to move my limbs. Floating in that void, my arms and legs thrashed uselessly, struggling to find any sort of purchase that would allow me to be grounded once more.

I finally calmed myself in the dream long enough to open my eyes and take in my surroundings. I was no longer in an empty void, I was floating in the vastness of space itself. Distant stars circled around me, and the nearest galaxy was vibrant with hues of purple and blue. However, as I stared into that void, I became aware of a terrifying realization: the Void was staring back. Two of the largest stars in my field of vision were pupils in the eyes of something so incomprehensibly large I was unable to take see it without panning my head a full 180-degrees. As the eyes stared back at me, directly at me, only one word entered my mind.

The Void seemed to say, "COME."

I bolted upright in my bed in a pool of sweat. My lungs burned, and I gasped for air. I turned to the chronometer on my bunk side table. Six minutes had passed since I had fallen asleep. I realized this was the dream Emmylou was talking about.

Shaking my head, I attempted to shake off the feeling of dread. Easier said than done. I manage to fall back asleep relatively quickly and was immediately thrust back into the dream. Same as before, same six minutes, same primal feel upon waking. It was like watching a movie with a toddler who only wanted to see their favorite part over and over again.

This continued for sixteen dream cycles until I finally gave up. I decided if I wasn't sleeping I might as well be working, although I realized I should report this to Doctor Yang first.

I strode down the corridor toward Psychiatry, still bleary-eyed and groggy, trying my best to avoid the black puddles of sap forming faster than the increasingly ragged custodial team could clean. As I rounded the corner to the hallway in which the office was located, raised voices and a jostling crowd greeted me. I hurried my pace and put on my best Captain's voice, shaken as it currently was.

"What's going on here?!" I boomed and tried to hide my surprise when it actually worked. The mob stopped immediately and looked at me. Suddenly bashful, their eyes could not meet mine. "Well?" I questioned.

A meek voice from the back arose. "It's the psychiatrist, sir. Dr. Yang won't give us sleep-aids." A murmur of validation from the crowd followed the statement.

A pair of terrified eyes peeked from the inside of the office. Recognizing them as the aforementioned Yang, I realized my stupidity. I had a ship full of terrified, sleep-deprived people, and I sent them to one person who was supposed to solve all of their problems. What was I thinking?

Regardless, I had to get this under control.

"Why do you all need something to help you fall asleep? Just go to sleep. It's always night around here." This joke didn't land, either.

"It's the dream, sir," a different voice answered. "None of us can sleep because of that damn dream."

Even though I knew it was coming, my blood ran cold. The dream had actually "spread" throughout the ship as Dr. Marren warned me. This would cause panic, and that's the last thing we needed.

"Unfortunately, the message sent a short time ago was sent in error. Upon further research, with sleep-aids in your system, your breathing could become so shallow, given the lower oxygen in the Magna lately, it could be dangerous." A lie, a terrible lie, illogical and stupid even, here I was contradicting my own instructions to the department heads, but I needed these people to remain calm.

Knowing their alternative to the dream was asphyxiation seemed to pacify the mob. I continued, "I know this dream is an aggravation, but there is nothing we can do about it. It is only a dream. Do your best to try and get some rest. You'll need it in the coming days. Dismissed to your quarters."

The order seemed to snap them from any dissenting thoughts, and the crowd dispersed. An obviously shaken Dr. Yang gave me a thorough tongue lashing for making such a stupid call, but she took note on my having the dream as well. Moving away from her office, I could feel the weight of exhaustion seeping in, but I had work to do.

Relative civility lasted eight more days. With a mere forty-eight hours of oxygen left, extreme conservation measures were put into place. Unnecessary crew decks were closed off and inhabitants evacuated to common areas to conserve oxygen. This meant the majority of the crew and their families were crammed into a few decks.

Unfortunately, this would light the fire that would burn the whole ship down.

My singular mind became getting into the automated systems and stopping the injections of glyphosate so the tree could heal itself. IBSEA had some of the best computer scientists in the world at their disposal, and it showed. We were making progress but slow progress. I still received reports from an increasingly bedraggled Dr. Marren, but I barely gave them any heed. She mentioned something about small fights over space and oxygen, a few dead bodies, and a group of psychosis riddled crew who formed a cult-like group called "The Dreamers." They were seeking to hasten the death of the tree as it would let them "ascend" when it died. I would respond with a "dismissed" without looking away from the screen.

The biggest annoyance, however, was the hallucinations impeding my work. Blaming it on a lack of sleep, I began to hear the dream's command "COME" all the time. Like a low rumbling drum, always beating away its steady funeral dirge in my head, "COME. COME. COME. COME." I tried my best to block it out but found my thoughts increasingly scattered.

I was so close, a mere few encryptions remained for me to break through, and I would have saved us all.

A panicked banging against my locked door snapped me from my computer screen. I vaguely heard the shouts of who I guessed was Emmylou and maybe Dr. Yang, but thought they could wait, I was just about to get in.

Thankfully, the Magna's emergency alert alarm began sounding in the ship's intercoms, a grotesque *weeeeeeeeooooouuuwww* droning on and on. I took this as the small blessing because it helped drown out the screams emanating from outside my door and did wonders to quiet the incessant "COME. COME. COME" in my ears.

With a final keystroke, the last encryption screen fell away, and I accessed the automated systems. There was an issue, though. I was met with a nearly empty computer file, save for one singular video. At the end of my rope, I ran the video.

The video player popped up on screen and the video began:

"Good day, sir or madam! My name is Richard Crawlsey, and you should feel very special for many reasons, but one in particular!" Crawlsey was a well-dressed man in his early fifties with slicked back hair. He wore a suit worth more money than I had ever made in my adult life. I recognized him immediately, the CEO of the International Biological Space Exploration Association. The video continued.

"You and your crew have been selected to fulfill the most important role any one human could be part of. You get to be part of "The Feeding!" He paused to adjust his tie. "You may be asking yourself, what in the world is The Feeding? Well, I am here to tell you.

"Many years ago, long before IBSEA was a global powerhouse, we learned of a creature in the deep reaches of space. We called it 'The Dream Void.'" Winking at the camera, he added, "By now, I'm sure you know why it has that name. Terrifying, isn't it?"

Crawsley's Cheshire cat grin never left his face. "Now, how we came upon this information is not important for your purposes. What is important to you and your crew is what we learned. The Dream Void is VERY hungry and traveling on a collision course with Earth. It fell to us to become its zookeepers and feed the big ol' guy."

An artist's rendering flashed on screen. It was indeed the face from the dreams. A massive creature with eyes that shone like stars, or that were stars, I couldn't really tell.

"You lucky cattle get to keep the Earth safe for another day," he chuckled. "You see, when the DV (as we call him) constantly eats, and its peculiar specifications are met, it doesn't move. As long as we keep sending organic material its way, it will stay where it is, never harming a soul."

Crawlsey moved to sit in a chair and continued, "Here's the problem. Ol' DV only enjoys organic material if it is suffering from mental duress. It emanates a field of horror to affect anyone within range, but that doesn't always do it. So, we had to give a little insurance with the whole tree poisoning. Isn't that fascinate—"

I shut the video off. I had seen enough.

Not only were we dead, we never had a chance. I leaned back in my chair and closed my eyes. It was entirely too much for my addled brain to process.

The computer screen flickered to life with a new warning message. It read: Final feeding preparations commencing. A boost of speed propelled the Magna forward, and the ship began to shake.

I decided to take this chance to perform my duties as a Captain. Better late than never, I suppose. The door slid open to reveal an absolute massacre. The blaring of the alarm, coupled with the red flashing lights of the emergency system, almost helped hide the bloodstains smearing the wall. Almost. The word "COME" was written over and over in overlapping chaos. Bodies were strewn about the corridor.

My heart sank when I saw Emmylou Marren and Patricia Yang among the corpses. I was saddened, of course, but learning what I had just learned, they were ahead of the curve.

Some of the bodies were garbed in a bastardization of the standard Magna uniform. The Magna jumpsuit had been ripped and torn into a ragtag robe complete with hood that covered the face. *Must be The*

Dreamers, I thought and moved past the scene, neglecting the pools of blood mixing with black sap from the trees.

Somehow, I found myself in the Arboretum. It was more of the same as the hallway. Bodies littering the grass, draped over swings that children used to play on, and discarded in combative piles like yesterday's action figures. My eyes finally fell upon the Magna Tree itself. It was dead. Finally, sourly dead. There was one change, though. With a quick glance, one would think there were macabre Halloween decorations on the tree. Upon closer inspection, it was clear to see the decorations were The Dreamers. Robes draped from corpses hung from branches somehow managing to hold their body weight.

Unable to process the atrocity, I found myself a spot at the base of the tree and stared at nothing. It felt nice to not think about anything, even for a moment. I thought I was ready for it to be over, and soon, parts began to fall away from the exterior of the ship while the ship increased in speed, causing the bodies to swing and tangle in the branches above me.

After what felt like an eternity, the floor finally fell out from under me. I dropped into the void of space, keeping my forward momentum. A cursory glance showed I was one of the few that had survived up to that point, but it didn't matter much longer. My eyes narrowed ahead of me, and there they were. The two star-like pupils watched the bodies floating through space.

The voice in my head was ravenous, screaming manically.

COMECOMECOMECOMECOMECOME.

I thought I was ready to die, but as I watched the massive maw of this incomprehensible creature open to consume me, I knew I was wrong.

I opened my mouth and tried my best to scream.

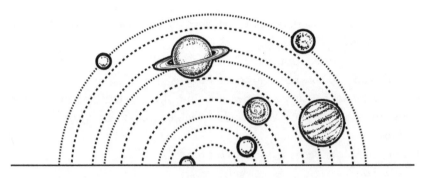

Utsuhi

By Fidel E. Arévalo León

H*i.*

"Hello?"

Who are you?

"I—"

Wait, hold on. There is no way you could give me an interesting answer. At least, not as interesting as if I were to ask where the hell you came from.

"Come from? That's a really, really long story. Not to mention angst-ridden. Trust me, you don't want to know. Besides, I'm more concerned about where I ended up this time."

You mean you don't know where you are? Is that why you decided to crash land in such a spectacular way?

"What? No. I—didn't actually choose to do that. I'm a traveler. I was flying through this area, most of which is uncharted territory, and this planet caught my attention. When I approached it—I don't know, I must have miscalculated the planet's gravity. It was stronger than I expected.

Which, come to think of, is not the first time something like this has happened."

You are a traveler? And you don't know where you are?

"Correct."

And you've crash-landed by accident? Which, apparently, is something that happens to you often?

"Well, not often, but...yeah."

You, um...You are not a very good traveler, are you?

"Hey! That's just, you know, the kind of complications that come with traveling. Anyway, why would I decide to crash land just because I'm lost?"

I don't know. Because it sounds like fun?

"... Fun?"

Yup. Besides, if you are lost and you suddenly crash land, you've solved your problem. It means you have gotten somewhere.

"That doesn't make any sense."

Who says it has to make sense? In any case, whether you decided to crash land for fun or not, it looks like your spaceship has seen better days.

"I guess you could say that. Fortunately, I don't think it's beyond repair. Putting it back together is probably going to take some time."

Definitely. Seems like you are going to be stuck here for a while. What should I call you?

"What should you call me? That's a bit complicated, too. If you are asking for my name, then I don't think there is a name that belongs to me anymore."

Really? Huh. Is that because of your ridiculously angst-ridden past? Wow. It must have been bad if you don't want to tell people your name now.

"Heh... Ok, fair enough. Let's forget about the angst. I guess S.T. is still something I could answer to."

Stee? Huh. Okay, Stee. Welcome to Utsuhi, the world of the blue stones.

"Right. Good to know...Anyway, don't get me wrong, it's been a pleasant conversation so far, but my spaceship is still on fire. Do you think you could help me put it out? I figured it would have died out by now, but I guess I was carrying more flammable material than I expected."

Oh! Yeah, sure. Do you really want to do that, though? Your spaceship looks so awesome covered in flames.

"I know, but I learned a long time ago flying through space and having stuff on fire are two things that don't go well together."

Stee, I think it looked better when it was on fire.

"I know, right? Like I said, though, if there is one thing experience has taught me, it's usually not a good idea to fly spaceships when they are in flames, regardless of how awesome you think they might look."

Why not?

"They tend to explode after a while. Explosions are pretty cool, but they are harder to survive than crash landings."

You know that from experience too?

"Yup. There is no use trying to fix this thing while it's still smoking. Why don't you tell me more about this world? It was... Utsuhi, right? You weren't kidding about the stones. I could see them from space, like blue stars over the white sand. It drew my attention to this planet."

You want some? I'm sure no one would notice if they were gone.

"Um... Maybe later? It's not like I can do anything with them right now, besides adding them to the charred heap holding all my earthly possessions."

Really? I can think of a bunch of things you could do with an endless supply of blue stones. I mean, you could juggle them? You could make a fortress with them? And maybe... Ok, no, I guess that's it.

"What do you usually do with them?"

Not much. I don't like them.

"No? Why not?"

It's a long story. Hey, just like yours! Don't you think it impolite to blindside newly arrived visitors with overly long stories?

"I'm not sure normal standards of politeness apply for unannounced, crash landing visitors. In fact, I'm pretty sure you would be well within you rights to kick me off the planet if you wish."

Nonsense! Besides, we established you didn't crash land on purpose, right?

"Huh? Yes, but I still—"

See? Not your fault. C'mon, it's getting late, and you should rest before trying any repairs. I'll show you somewhere you can sleep.

———————

This is it, Stee. Looks comfy, doesn't it?

"This is a tree."

Wrong—This is The Tree. As in, the only one.

"Really? The only one around here?"

The only one in Utsuhi, as far as I know. I haven't gotten around checking every nook and cranny of this planet, so I guess there could still be another one.

"Don't get me wrong, but when you mentioned a place to rest, I imagined something with—I don't know— a roof, maybe?"

Oh! Yeah, I see how you might expect that. I know it isn't much, Stee, but trust me, leaning on the tree is more comfortable than sleeping flat on the sand. Besides, it's probably not going to rain anytime soon. There would have to be clouds for that to happen.

"No, I mean, it's just that I don't get it. I thought there would be something built, some sign of people living here—But there is nothing. Just the sand and the stones and the tree...and you. Are we that far from towns and cities, from civilization? From where your people live?"

There are no such things.

"What's going on? Where is everyone else?"

Isn't it obvious? The monsters ate them.

"There are people-eating monsters on this planet?!"

Heh heh...You should see the look on your face! Nah, I'm just kidding. Everyone left a long time ago. It's just me. But don't worry, we are safe. You should really get some sleep. You have lots of work to do.

"Ok. But, wait. There aren't monsters around here?"

Not anymore. I ate them.

"Oh. You mean—"

Heh heh... Your face. C'mon, it's just too easy!

———————————

How does it look?

"I don't think the spaceship was quite so... bent before. It really isn't as bad as it could have been.

In fact, I think most of the damage had been done long before the crash landing."

Really? And you hadn't noticed? When was the last time you gave it any sort of maintenance?

"Never?"

... Right. You must be the worst traveler ever.

"Hey! This ship has turned out to be surprisingly sturdy. It has never seemed to be in need of repairs."

Where you going to wait for it to blow up before checking if it was working properly?

"That's the thing, actually. I know this spaceship is old, and I've wanted to replace it for quite some time. However, when I come across a planet with a spaceship on it I can 'borrow'—"

"Borrow?"

"Well, you know, I took them? As far as I could tell, they didn't have an owner."

You just stole them?

"No! Every time I find an abandoned spaceship, I try to see if anyone will claim it. Nevertheless, I have never found them. And I've never understood why, since logically someone must have brought it there, or at least someone must have built it. In any case, considering the lack of owner, I have taken the ships, but only because I need a replacement."

How come you're still using this one?

"It's the only one that has survived this long. See, every other spaceship I have tried has broken down soon afterwards, and that's when they don't suddenly explode outright. This one has turned out to be surprisingly sturdy."

I'd say it is rather flexible, too.

"Not to mention flammable. Seriously, I've lost track of how many times this thing has burst into flames."

Yup. Definitely the worst traveler ever.

"How long have you been on your own?"

I'm not on my own. I've had the tree and the stars to keep me company. Oh, and I guess there were the monsters, too, but they were too delicious.

"Right... Why are you the only one here? How come there isn't anyone else around?"

Those are two very different questions, but let's see, I'm sure you've noticed Utsuhi is a very unusual place.

"Now that you mentioned it, I'm not sure how you can tell when it's getting late. I haven't seen a sun in all the time I've been here. You can see the stars all of the time, but it is never dark. It's like the sand and the stones emit a light of their own. Frankly, it's more than a little—"

It's annoying, isn't? All that light, all of the time?

"Not at all. I was going to say it's breathtaking. It's beautiful."

Yeah, I guess. I don't think I can appreciate it after all this time.

"You don't think it's beautiful?"

No, it is pretty. In its own way. But, anyhow, you surely noticed something else?

"Other than a monster-eating girl living here all alone? No, not really."

"C'mon, Stee! You must have seen from space there is no water among all this sand.

"Not even underground?"

Not much. It's more than enough for me. When the oceans and rivers started to dry out, my people realized they would no longer be able to survive. They decided to move to another planet, far away.

"I see. But what about you? Why didn't you go with them?"

I... I just couldn't.

"Why not?"

It...wasn't really a choice. I just can't leave all this behind.

"All of this? You mean your home world?"

This tree, this sky—it is the only home I've known. If I left, I might never find them again.

"But aren't you lonely? Haven't you considered leaving this place?"

I thought if anyone would understand, Stee, it would be you. Isn't traveling on your own lonely? And yet, I doubt is a decision you second-guess.

"You might be right. But the strange thing is, we seem to have done completely different things for the exact same reasons."

What do you mean?

"I, too, feel like I haven't had a choice about the decisions I've made. I did what I had to do to be true to myself. You decided to stay, but I left my home world without a second thought—precisely because I couldn't call it home anymore. Now that I think about it, you're very lucky to have a place like this one."

Lucky. And with a bunch of yummy monsters.

"Heh... It looks like I'm going to be shipwrecked for a while, so I guess I'll keep you company. I've given thought to your idea of making a fortress with the blue stones, and it sounds like it would be fun. Do you want to give it a shot?

Bleugh! That would be one horrible fortress... Although it does sound like fun. But, no... We can't. You need to hurry.

"Hurry?"

You need to fix your spaceship. It's getting late.

"I'm not sure the engine is supposed to have this many holes. Then again, I'm not sure it would be a good idea to cover them up. What should I do?"

Perhaps they are the reason your spaceship hasn't blown up yet.

"I don't think the ominous creaking sound the ship does once in a while was quite so ominous before. It's always been there, as far as I can remember. It can't be that bad."

Hey, Stee? Where are you traveling to, anyway? Are you looking for a new home?

"Nah, I gave up on that a long time ago. That was the reason I left my home world in the first place—I believed I could find a home somewhere else. I turned out to be very wrong, so I kept looking. I can't say that's what I'm doing anymore."

What are you looking for now?

"I... I don't know. It feels like I'm searching because I don't have anything else."

That can't be true.

"Huh?"

All journeys must come to an end. That is what defines them. That is what drives the traveler. The end is not necessarily a place. It could be a person, or an experience, or an idea. But if there is nothing, the journey becomes aimless wandering.

"Well, maybe that's what happened to me."

That's not possible. You said you came to Utsuhi because something caught your attention. That proves you are still looking for something—Something that, even if just for an instant, you thought you might find here.

"You are making a lot of conjectures."

Am I wrong?

"I'm... not sure. I've never thought about it that way. Besides, if my journey ends by being eaten by a monster, I don't think there is much use worrying about it."

Oh, that's not the point. I seriously doubt you want to be eaten by a monster. The real question is, what do you really want?

...

Don't worry, you don't have to tell me. But don't play dumb with me. I know you have some idea. You are not as good a liar as you think you are.

"Heh. From the sound of things, you seem to know the answers to the questions you are asking me."

Nah, I'm not that good. You just haven't had anyone to talk to for far too long.

———————

"I don't think you really answered my question."

Which one?

"Have you thought about leaving this place? You told me you couldn't, but have you never thought about it?"

I have. It's just...complicated. Like I said, this is my home world, and I don't exactly have a spaceship lying around. My people took them all with them.

"Why? That is so unnecessarily callous. Were they trying to punish you or something?"

Not at all. I didn't ask them to leave one behind.

"Okay, but that's not what I mean. I didn't ask whether you considered the matter in purely practical terms. It's more about what you asked me a while ago. What do you want? Do you still want to stay on this planet after all this time?"

I can't answer that question.

"Huh? I just—"

I mean, who the hell do you think you are, Stee? You just got here, and you think you already know all there is to know about me, about this world? You think it's okay to crash land and disturb my peace, a peace that has cost me so much to achieve, to come to terms with my own existence?

"No—I'm sorry, it's not like that at all. I didn't mean to upset you—I just don't get it. In spite of what you say, you don't seem that attached to this planet, and—Is it just me, or have more blue stones appeared since I arrived?"

I'm sorry. I didn't mean to burst out like that. Look, I admit I haven't been entirely honest with you, but I really can't leave this world. I can't. And I didn't think anyone would come before... before it was too late.

"What—"

You should focus on getting yourself out of here. C'mon, it's getting late. You should get some sleep. You need to hurry."

"You know, I just realized you still haven't told me your name."

No? I'm pretty sure I have.

"I'm pretty sure you haven't. I think I would remember something like that."

Oh, no, I did. You weren't paying attention.

"Do you think you could tell me again?"

Nuh-huh. If you don't remember, I'm sure you'll figure it out eventually.

"If you change your mind, you know you can come with me when I fix my spaceship, right?"

I know. I never doubted it for a second.

Stee, were you serious about what you said?

"What did I say?"

You said I didn't seem to be emotionally attached to this world. Why do you think that?

"I've noticed where your eyes wander."

Hmm?

"Compared to my home world, you have no idea how peaceful this planet is. I was born in a constant, massive sandstorm. We had no choice but to live underground. And yet, I knew what the sky looked like. My people had figured out ways to travel to the moons. Nevertheless, the surface of the world itself was inhospitable. We certainly could not walk on it like we are doing right now."

... Right.

"Because of that, when I take in the landscape of this planet, I look straight ahead. I gaze at the glowing sand, at the blue stones, and at the horizon—the place where the distant hills meet the sky. It's something I never could have done back in my home world. You, on the other hand... You have told me so many times how important this place is to you, yet

47

when you let your eyes wander, when you contemplate your surroundings—when you think I'm sleeping—you look upwards. You look to the stars above. It's almost as if you are wondering if there is someone out there, looking back."

What makes you say that?

"Back when I was looking for a home, I used to lie down in the countless empty planets I found, and ask myself if there was someone looking back. Now I wonder if you were the one looking at me."

Nah, it's nothing quite so convoluted. It's just important to look at the stars every once in a while.

"Is that so? Why?"

They remind you there is an entire universe out there, far beyond our reach... I was asking because I got a similar impression of you. Namely, that you don't seem to particularly care for your spaceship.

"Really?"

You've been doing this traveling thing for a while, and you never checked your ship for damages. On top of that, in all this time I've watched you repair your spaceship, you seem to regard it and refer to it in a cold and detached way, as if it were little more than a tool that gets you around. I thought travelers were not quite so indifferent towards their means of transportation.

"I've never really thought about it. You might be right. It probably has to do with the fact the ship is a little bit stolen."

A little bit stolen? You stole it a little bit?

"A tiny bit. Back in my home world, this was one of the ships we used to get to the moons—Pretty much anyone could use them at any time. There was an unspoken understanding you were not supposed to take them out of orbit. When it came time to escape, I didn't have any other means of leaving the planet. I guess that's why I've never felt the ship belongs to me."

Escape? You had to escape your home world.

"In a manner of speaking. It seemed like an outrageous idea at the time. As far as I knew, no one else had left before. I was afraid, because even though I had to escape, I also knew I would never go back."

Oh, I'm sure you'll go back some day.

"Huh? Why?"

Isn't it obvious? To return the spaceship, of course.

"Heh... Right. If I manage to make it fly again."

You will. And you need to hurry.

"Could you tell me what your people were like, before they left?"

That's an extremely vague question, Stee. Why do you ask?

"I'm amazed there is absolutely no sign of them. If I hadn't found you, I would have thought that this planet never harbored life. Just tell me something about them—Were they kind-hearted? Were they distrustful? Were they naive? Were they satisfied with their lot in life? What impression did you have of them?"

I don't think it's possible to make generalizations about them. The truth is, I didn't know them very well.

"No?"

Or... maybe I did? My first real memory of waking up is after they left. I might have a vague idea of what they were like, but other than that, I'm as curious about them as you are.

"You don't remember them?"

No, I... I do remember. It's hard to explain. The time they were here is like a distant dream from which I woke up a long time ago.

"But, what do you recall?"

I can't say I understand them, much less identify with them. And I would be lying if I said that I missed them.

"Is that why you don't regret not going with them?"

I guess so. I didn't belong among them.

"What made you and them so irrevocably different?"

They had a bizarre perspective on life. Too simplistic—Or, perhaps it is more accurate to say, too escapist—for its own good. Let me tell you a story that was passed down from generation to generation. As you'll see, it is an important story, because it tells the myth of how Utsuhi was created.

"Right."

As the story goes, one day a girl was born... Or, wait, did she fall from the stars? It was something like that, but the point is, she was alone. She created the ground and the sky, wind and the rivers—you know, before they were gone—the light and the darkness. She wandered the planet as she killed time creating, or something along those lines...

But she was lonely, lonelier that you can imagine. Her loneliness eventually turned into anger, and her anger was so great it acquired a life of its own, a being in itself. This being burned the world to ashes, and the ashes turned into the glowing sand you see here. According to the myth, the sand glows with her anger, but the light is what allows life to grow, in spite of there being no sun nearby.

"... Okay. The story is a bit odd, I admit, but I don't see the problem."

Don't you get it? The people that lived here, they were like the girl. Like her, they couldn't deal with loneliness. They ran away from fear, pain, sadness—anything remotely unpleasant. They went to great lengths to keep it at bay, and their lives were all the poorer for it.

"Don't you think that's normal?"

Screw normal! Life can't just be about happiness. Hardship is the only thing that can give meaning to victory! If you keep away all the suffering, then you are mutilating your own existence. Don't you think so? Don't you think, if you don't understand that everything must come to an end, you'll only be the shadow of a shadow of what you could have been?

"Yeah. I think so."

Well, they didn't. They always ran away from pain. They couldn't appreciate the worth, the preciousness of a good ending. And... And they left Utsuhi, long before it was truly necessary. They didn't even try. They couldn't be bothered to deal with it, to try and find a way to save their own world.

"I see. I'm sorry. You know, you sound a lot like the girl from the story."

Heh... That detail is not lost on me. But I'm definitely not her.

"You sure? How do you know?"

Because I am not angry.

"No?"

No. Not anymore.

———

...That's the secret to making the most delicious, rich-flavored kind of monster soup. If you are going to barbecue it, the preparations have to be a little different. First of all, you need—"

"I can't stay here, can I?

What? You mean—

"I know something is going on. There are definitely more blue stones than when I first arrived. Even the sand seems to be glowing brighter... And you keep telling me to hurry."

...

"I've been thinking I could stay on this planet for a while—"

No! No, Stee... You can't.
"Why?"

...

"I remember what you asked me. About why I keep traveling."
... And?
"It's been so long, I put it out of my mind. What I truly wanted, the reason I kept traveling after giving up on a home, was because... because I wished to find someone else."
Someone else?
"Yes...In my travels, in the countless of planets I've been to, I've found all sorts things: cities, palaces, roads, aqueducts, even spaceships from the most primitive to the most impossibly complex. There are relics of civilizations scattered all over the universe. But the civilizations themselves, the people... They are nowhere to be found. That's why I could never find a place where I belonged. All I came across was a bunch of empty buildings. There was no one I could make a connection with. Before I came here, I had known of no world that had sentient life forms."

...

"I mean, even the people of my home world were like yours; mere shadows of shadows of their own selves, mindlessly carrying on their routines from day-to-day. I never felt they were truly alive. Even though I gave up on finding a home, the question remained: why wasn't I able to find anyone else? Was it possible there were no other worlds with life in the universe?"
I see.
"And now I've found you. It was so natural, so sudden the way I met you after the crash landing. At first, I didn't realize I had finally found what I was looking for—something I had almost forgotten about. I don't get why, of all places, you had to be in the one world that has absolutely no traces of any civilization. I don't understand—But I don't care either. I just don't care."
Stee...
"I would stay here. I really would. This is... one of the most breathtakingly beautiful worlds I've ever been to. But—there is something far worse than dried out water supplies going on here, isn't it?"
Yes... There is.
"What is it?"

It's true the planet was evacuated after the rivers and oceans were gone. But, that's not why everyone left. The truth is Utsuhi used to be a much larger planet.

"What? You mean that—"

It started when the blue stones began to appear. The seemed to be harmless enough, and they were certainly pretty; so even though no one could explain their presence, no one really paid them much mind. Soon enough, strange changes started happening around the world. The land became distorted. The wind patterns became erratic. The water started disappearing. Suddenly, entire areas started to disappear with piles of blue stones left in their wake. In fact, in all the places where bizarre events happened, the blue stones increased in numbers.

"What does it mean?"

I'm not sure what the stones are—crystallized sand, perhaps? — but, by the time it was obvious what was going on, the evacuation was ordered. No attempt was made to understand the phenomenon or reverse it. I doubt it can be reversed, in any case. But no, they just left.

"You mean...?"

Yes, Stee. Utsuhi is dying—It's disintegrating.

"Wow. It's far worse than I imagined."

It really is, isn't it? Although, I'm surprised no planets have blown up on you yet.

"No, they have—a couple of them. But this is very different. How much time do we have left?"

I'm not sure. I think it's safe, but it can't be much longer now. The planet is a fraction of the size it used to be, and I doubt the sand suddenly glowing with more intensity is a good sign. You really need to hurry.

"Right. But I don't understand—Why hadn't you told me any of this before?"

Honestly? I figured you would fix your spaceship long before lack of time became an issue— I never would have imagined you would ever wish to stay on this desolate planet. Believe me, the fact that you managed to come right before the planet imploded means you have the worst luck ever.

"It's not desolate."

Oh, it definitely is. The biggest reason I didn't want to tell you was because I knew you wouldn't understand why I'm going to stay here.

"What?! You are going to stay? But the planet is going to be destroyed!"

It is.

"But why? It's insane!"

It's because...I have lost my name.

"What does that have to do with—"

Look, Stee... I have to go. I'll be back soon. Maybe in a couple of days. Trust me, I have to take care of something very, very important. I'll see you in a bit, okay?

"Huh? Wait, hold on—"

You're almost done with repairs, right? Okay, how about this, if promise I'll go with you, will you promise to have your ship fixed by the time I come back?

"Really? You might..."

Just promise!

"Ok. I will."

All right... Good. I'll see you soon, Stee.

Hi.

"Hey. I was starting to think I wasn't going to see you again."

Don't you know a monster-eater's word can be trusted? I did say I would be back soon-ish.

"You aren't coming with me, are you?"

No.

"Why?"

There is not much time left. Utsuhi is starting to break up. It might be best if you didn't know.

"Please. I can't just leave you to die here. If you really want me to leave, then at least—"

I'm not like you, Stee. I'm not the 'someone else' you've been looking for. You need to understand, Stee, that...I'm not real.

"... What?"

My people were not very good at dealing with loss or death. They figured out a way to go on living, so to speak, after their bodies could no longer function. They created constructs that could be imprinted with a person's personality and memories. That way, no one would ever have to mourn or miss that person, and everyone could pretend they were still there.

"You mean...?"

I am one of such constructs.

"You?"

All the constructs were taken during the evacuation, so I don't know why I was left behind. Maybe I was forgotten. Maybe I was created by accident. Or maybe

I was left on purpose, to warn anyone that came here about what was going on. In any case, all that I know is when I first woke, everyone was gone, and I only had vague, foreign memories of how things had come to be.

"You're a construct? I don't care—You are the most real thing I have found in this universe. Why would you think that would bother me?"

Stee, I never thought it would bother you. That is not the problem.

"Then...?"

I am anchored to the planet. I am bound to its energy, to its fate, and that's how constructs exist. Anchors have a limited range. If I leave on your spaceship, I'll disappear before we escape the atmosphere.

"Are you—"

Yes, I'm sure. In fact, I went to check, one last time. If I walk far enough from here, I start to vanish. It happened this time, too... just like the others. Just as expected... Nothing has changed.

"But... But you said your people took the constructs with them! Why can't we do the same? Why can't we take your anchor?"

Oh, you really think of everything, don't you? I'm not sure where my anchor point is. I think it's near the tree, but I'm not sure. And, even if I knew, the technology to move anchor points is long gone. Anchors are not tangible, physical objects that can be touched. I am not something you can carry in your hands.

"This is terrible. Why...?"

Heh heh. Don't be silly, Stee. It's not terrible, and there is no reason. That's just the way things are.

...

Listen to me, Stee, and please remember this. It is very important.

"Yes?"

I am not sad. I am not angry. I am not afraid. And I am definitely not imprisoned here—I refuse to be imprisoned here. My fate might be bound to Utsuhi, but my actions, my choices, and my kindness, they are still my own. They are my freedom. Nothing can ever, ever take that away from me.

...

Only you and I exist on this planet. There is nothing else. Nothing but our words. When you leave, it will be your memories that will make me real.

"That... doesn't make any sense."

Who says it has to make any sense? Trust me, you will understand it in time. It'll come to you when you need it most.

"Why—Why don't we give it a shot? Come with me, and maybe—"

There is no point, Stee. Besides, I don't want to vanish yet. Long ago, I decided I would see this through, that I would make it until the end. That I wouldn't walk away into oblivion. Unlike others, I do appreciate a good ending.

"Then... I'll do the same. I'll stay with you."

What?

"I'll stay here. I'll see the end with you. I wouldn't be able to live with myself if—"

Have you listened to a word I said? Would you dishonor me in such a way?

"No! I... What? How—"

I have no one else to remember me, Stee, other than you! Will you let yourself die, and let my memory die with you, just because it's too freaking hard? Will you throw my last will—my wish—

to make sure you'll safely escape in time?

"I... I don't know what to do."

... Here. I almost forgot.

"... Huh?"

I have something for you.

"A blue stone?"

Yes. It's... the only one I've found that isn't completely hideous. It's not exactly the same color as the others, see? Maybe it existed before any of this happened.

...

It used to be beyond the range of the anchor. I have seen it countless of times, but I was too afraid to reach for it. This last time, though... I managed to grab it quickly enough. I wanted you to have it.

"Why?"

Do you think you could please take it with you? And could you leave it in your home world, next time you visit?

"Of course. Anything you want. But why do you want me to do that?"

I don't know. I think I want a part of me to stay there.

"... I see. I promise."

———————

Go, Stee! You know there is not much time left!

"Yes, I know. It's just—You still haven't told me your name."

Oh... Oh! Right. Almost forgot about that one... See, the thing is, you need to give me one, Stee.

"What do you mean?"

See, I don't know the name of the person who created me. It is not among the memories she left me, for some reason... But I've realized, even if I knew, it would be her name, not mine. I could have given myself a name, but that is not the way it should be. Names are something must be given by others. Since there is no one else around, it is up to you to give me a name.

"I see. Let me think. How about—How about Azuhi?"

Azuhi?' Really? C'mon, that doesn't sound like me at all!

"No? Well, how about—"

—But I like it. It's beautiful.

...

I'm sorry if you thought this was the end of your journey. I really am. But you have a long way to go before you rest.

"It does seem that way, doesn't it? I wish you could make the journey with me."

Me too. But, don't worry. Even if I'm not there, I promise no monster is ever going to eat you.

"Heh... Really? You promise?"

I promise.

...

I'm grateful for all of this, you know? More than I could ever tell you. And I'm so glad you're such a bad traveler, that you ended up crash-landing here.

"I'm glad, too. I won't forget."

I know you won't. Good bye, Stee.

"... Good bye, Azuhi."

Epilogue

"This was not the end. There would be hard times, of course; but at that moment, as I watched the sunset, none of it seemed to matter. Most people spend their lives running away from pain—I ran towards it, whenever it was necessary. After all, no one promised me a bed of roses... Only beautiful sunsets."

-X

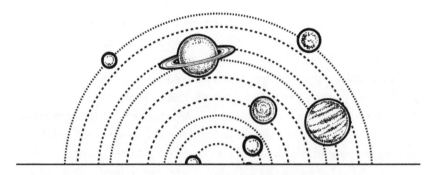

Forgotten Oasis

By McKay Wadsworth

I swallowed to relieve the burning dryness within my throat, but the itch of thirst persisted. Two long excruciating days had passed without a lick of water. Death only needed three days for my bones to be buried within the rolling hills of sand.

I pushed the hoverbike as hard as I could and held tight on the throttle as the old girl pitched and swayed. The loud *thoom* of her engine rose and fell as I shifted gears. Hovering over a large rock obscured within the sand, the entire chassis shook and grumbled. Then the engine choked and coughed as I made my way up a steep sandy slope. Once over the rise, the engine relaxed, and I came barreling in a nosedive down the dune's face. Red dust kicked out behind me as I emerged onto a flat barren waste.

Miles of the red rolling dunes finally came to an end. The sand beneath my bike changed from a dark red to a light beige as I entered a flat desert landscape. There were occasional crests of sand, but I could see the brown pointed peaks of the mountaintops in the distance obscured due to the high rising dunes.

Riding the endless waves had taken a toll on my white-toned fabric. My garments were stained by the red sand. Layers of wraps and shawls protected me from the burning heat of the sun as I sped across the flat landscape. Not an inch of skin could be seen on my person. The sun was one of many enemies in this dry forgotten world. Any loose clothing flapped behind me freely. My sun-tinted goggles protruded out of my headwrap; dust and grime battered against the lenses.

Suddenly, small silhouettes of what looked to be a person and another object came into view. The mirage of heat obscured fine details at this distance, but as I drew closer, it was clearly a man. I pulled gently on the brake. The blur of passing landscape slowed and the whipping winds died down, causing the heat of the glaring sun to catch up with me. The hoverbike's *thoom* receded back to a chugging pulse from the engine. I drifted slowly and came to an abrupt halt, staring at the lone stranger. The stranger didn't take any notice of me; he knelt in the sand covered in dirty gray robes, making repairs to his damaged ride.

"Heard yah comin' over the rise," he said.

"Yah?" I responded.

"If yer wantin' to rob me, I ain't got much. My bike's dead without charge. I have a couple of day's rations if yer interested, but that's about all I have of worth on me." He continued to work, not turning to face me.

"You armed?"

"Not at the moment. My blaster pistol is in its holster in my side bag on the bike. If yer gonna shoot me, now's the time."

"I don't plan on shootin' yah, old man."

"That's mighty generous of yah considering my current misfortune."

"What's wrong with the bike?"

He kicked the bike. "Battery's fried. The sumbitch can't give a solar charge without it shortin' out on me."

I chuckled. "That is unfortunate."

"Damn straight." He rose from the sand and turned to face me. The hood of his dirty robes attempted to obscure his dark gray curly hair but strands escaped into the sunlight. His face was withered, wrinkled, and tanned by the scorching sun. Dark bags lay strewn below his darker brown eyes. They appeared rougher than the sand itself. Below his eyes was a short, hooked nose that angled towards his mouth. The old man had a chiseled jawline that was covered with a light gray bushy beard. He smiled and bore his blackened grimy teeth.

He asked, "Yah gotta name?"

"Not one I'm willing to give."

He leaned back against his bike and started wiping the sweat of his brow with a muggy looking rag. "Yer smart not trustin' strangers."

"It's how I've stayed alive this long." I pulled out my pistol from my thigh holster and aimed it at him. He didn't flinch.

He smiled. "So yah are robbin' me?"

I nodded. "I didn't say otherwise. You say that pistol is in your side bag?"

He nodded.

"Unlatch that side bag and step away from your bike, if you wouldn't mind. No funny business. I hadn't planned on killing you, but if you make a jump for that blaster, you're as good as dead."

He unlatched the side bag and tossed it to the sand below before moving a couple yards away. I dismounted my bike and rummaged through his belongings. There wasn't much on him. Some rations, tools, and a knife. I slammed his bag to the ground. With a sudden surge of rage and gritty frustration, I screamed and kicked the bag across the sand.

A smile sprung to his cracked dry lips. He let out an old crackly laugh that was followed by a fit of coughs. "I know what yer lookin for, son."

I ignored him, returned to my bike, and started up the engine. The loud *thoom* bellowed through the empty landscape and echoed for miles.

The stranger suddenly darted toward me.

In an instant, I drew my pistol and aimed it at his old wrinkly forehead. He stopped in front of me and raised his empty hands in the air. I could smell his foul breath linger through my shawl and into my nose. His stupid smug expression vanished from his crusted lips. He trembled where he stood; loose sand from his hood sprinkling to the desert floor. There was sudden desperation in his brown sand eyes.

He spoke, taking careful consideration into every word he uttered from his crispy dry lips. "Yer searchin' for what everybody be searchin' for, and that be water. Ain't no point in denyin' it. I know where the water is, boy; I know of a spring."

The barrel of my blaster pushed deeper against his skull. "You're lying, old man."

He winced, "I ain't! I-I-swear to the founders, I know of a place."

I pressed the barrel deeper into his forehead.

"When was the last time yah had water, son? It's been a couple days for me. The spring ain't that far away from here. A day's drive if full on the throttle. Help me fix my bike, and I'll take yah there without any funny business. How does that sound?"

I lowered my sidearm. A circle from the barrel was left imprinted upon the wrinkly skin of his forehead. He relaxed and bore his blackened smile. "We have a deal?"

He reached his filthy hand towards me. I gave it a firm grasp. "We have a deal. But if you cross me, I'll end you quick, you understand?"

The man nodded. "Wouldn't expect it any other way."

I dismounted my bike and began to set up my tent. If I was going to help, I wasn't going to fix his junker in the heat of the midday sun. The old man helped me set up camp. All the while he talked and talked. Half of what he said I didn't hear, mostly because I chose not to listen.

Once the tent was staked, we had decent shade to work. I didn't bother fastening the tent's exterior walls, that could be done later. I laid a rug across the sand and sat down. With my tools by my side, I pried the rusted metal from his bike and dug inside the beast's innards for the dead battery. The old man's bike was an older model than my own. I took it apart, cursing under my breath. I couldn't believe it had lasted this long. Luckily, I had the parts to get his girl back to galloping pace.

"You don't have much time left in this bike of yours," I said with a greasy bolt in the side of my mouth. "Once I finish the battery, I guess you have a thousand more miles in her, at the least."

The man sighed. "I figured as much. Shame. I've become quite attached to her."

I screwed on the last panel and scoffed. "You're better off not making attachments in this world, old man. No sense in getting close to something you're going to lose."

The old man chuckled and gritted his dirtied teeth. "I suppose that means you ain't gonna tell me your name, right?"

"You got that straight. How did you come to know of a spring anyhow?"

He sat down and spoke without eyeing me. "It's complicated."

I began putting my tools back in my tool kit and said, "Enlighten me."

"I came across some folks talking about a place far west from here. I didn't believe em' at first. A whole spring for drinkin'? I've never heard such a thing. Too good to be true, ain't it? Them folks' words were so damn good, they sweet talked me into believin' em'."

"So we, and they, know of its location? Is that going to cause problems?"

"No. It's taken care of."

I stopped putting away my tools and drew out my pistol. He lifted up his hands once again, gave a hearty chuckle, and tried to lighten the mood. "You know, friend, you sure enjoy pointing that blaster at me."

"You killed 'em, didn't you?"

He nodded. "I reckon I did."

"What makes me think you won't kill me?"

"I have no intention on killin' yah, son."

"And how in the hell am I supposed to believe that?"

"Cuz yer thirsty, boy. When was the last time yah heard word of open water anywhere on this dry rock of ours?" He moved slowly towards me. "I'm dying of thirst just like you, son." The old man moved his forehead into the barrel of my blaster. "I killed them folks because I wanted to live!" His sand-like eyes pierced into my own. "I can see you have that same urge in yah as well. There is only so much sharin' one can do before that pretty pool of water is all drank up. Now look, as far as I know, I'm the only person that knows exactly where this spring is."

He removed his forehead from the barrel and slowly moved his head away from the blaster. "I ain't going to cross yah, I'm done with crossin.' I've come too far, sacrificed too much, just to have it sift through my fingers like a handful of sand. I can live with sharin' it with yah. You stopped and helped me, and you haven't killed me thus far. I'd say that's worth a reward, don't yah think?"

I held my blaster on him for what felt like a good while, then slowly, painfully holstered my weapon.

"We'll sleep through the rest of the day and leave at nightfall."

The old man nodded. "Like the sound of that. Cooler breeze, easier ride."

I pointed at his bike. "Get that thing out of here so we can get some rest!"

The old man quickly moved his outside the tent and parked it next to mine. He then helped me fasten the tent to provide us with extra shade for sleeping. After staking the walls deep into the sand, the air inside our shelter felt immediately cooler. I shook what sand had collected on my rug outside and laid it back inside the tent. It was soothing to feel something other than the gritty sand at our feet. Next, we both laid out our bedrolls. The old man took a spot in the corner, and I took another.

"Have a good rest, son."

I didn't respond, nor did I sleep. As I lay awake, I heard the old man breathing in and out; his breath was coarse and heavy. After coughs and adjustments, his breathing softened. Then he was suddenly taken, lost into desert dreams.

Light began to fade, losing itself behind the brown mountaintops. The Wind Mother began her nightly task of sweeping the sand, creating ripples and waves across the desert floor. Usually the sound brushing against the sand gave me comfort like my mother singing to me long ago. She would cradle me in her arms as she sang, and I would become lost in the safety of her embrace.

The lullabies of my new Wind Mother would do the same. She sang to me, and the sand would hug me, holding me tight against her dune breasts. The melody enticed my eyes to close and dream of mothers, both of sand and flesh, but not this time. No matter how much Wind Mother persisted, my eyes would not close. I lay awake, awaiting our departure.

Night came and a cool breeze gusted against the tent. It was time. I shook the old man awake. Groggily, he rolled up his bedroll and helped me take down the tent. I liked him tired; he was far less chatty. We started up our bikes. Mine roared awake. The old man's ride sputtered, choked, and joined in the song of roaring engines.

"Try to keep up!"

His voice carried over the deafening throng of our bikes, and he sped towards the mountains in the distance. I followed, keeping a close chase.

The cool breeze of the night was a welcome and blissful change compared to the blistering heat of the midday sun. I enjoyed feeling the cool wind beat across my chest as we rode at top speeds. The stars in the heavens and the light of the two moons gave us sight as we rode across the desert. The sand looked different at night. It wasn't blinding and looked more like a gentle blanket laying across the ground. I felt guilty riding through it, casting sand behind me as we cut through the wind mother's blanket like a sharp knife.

The large mountains towering peaks loomed over us as we drew close to them. They looked like massive giants with glaring eyes staring down upon us, questioning our presence into their lands. Our water lay hidden within the giants' piercing gaze. Would it be too much of an imposition to enter uninvited and drink their treasure? Others had done so. Others that the old man had willingly killed. What made us different from those that had entered the mountains before?

Evil. We were both stained with the marks of our sins; the mountains could see it and watched us with such distaste. I shook my head, trying to rid the feel of its piercing stare. Perhaps they always looked like this? Maybe the people that knew of the spring were evil themselves? I suppose it was best the old man did them off. A few less guns to worry about and a better chance to survive.

After half the night's travel was lost to us, the old man slowly came to a stop. Up ahead lay the dry mountains and their sharp cliffs.

"See that?"

A faint orange hue of light flickered against the rocks. "Fire? I thought you said we were the only ones who knew about the spring?"

"Guess I was wrong." He looked at me and smirked. "That happens from time to time, kid. What I want to know is, who's got the stones to light an open fire at this time of night?"

"It can't be just one person. No one's that stupid. It has to be a clan."

"A clan, huh?" The old man gave a deep sigh. "I say we check it out, see what we're dealin' with. I've come too far to turn back now."

He sped towards the cliffs, and I followed behind. We cut our engines before reaching the cliffside and pushed our bikes up the sharp cliffs. I led the way and the old man followed, slipping and cursing with every misstep. He took notice of my footholds and handholds as we progressed, and his slipping and cursing became less frequent.

Finally, I pulled myself where the orange flickering light illuminated the cliff edge. I took the old man's hand and pulled him up by my side. He rolled over on his back; his breath was heavy, and he wheezed with a smile. "Well shit. I could use a sip of water. What about yourself?" He let out a hearty cackling laugh which led into a coughing fit. I helped him to his feet and patiently waited for him to compose himself. We then ventured into the rocks following the orange glow of light. The old man led the way, and I kept my blaster pistol within reach.

We followed a tunnel inside the cliffs where the faint orange light bounced off of the sandstone rock. The rocks began to change the further we went. The sandstone was replaced with a smooth limestone. The air suddenly became cool, heavy, and even damp as we delved further into the mountain. The old man stopped and brushed his dirtied finger against the side wall. He licked his finger. "Moisture. We must be gettin' close."

The light grew brighter until suddenly a massive cavern opened up to us. Stalactites hung draped upon the cavern ceiling like long pointed teeth within the mouth of a beast. From the tips of the stalactite's teeth, drips of the precious moisture fell into a pool below, creating a heavenly echo that bounced off the walls and into our ears.

Before us lay a large pool of water. We dove to the spring's edge and began lapping water into our mouths.

Drinking the heavenly liquid felt like quenching a raging fire inside of me. The water soothed my dry throat, causing my body to return to its long-awaited ease. The spring was larger than I anticipated. The moisture collected could easily provide for more than a hundred lives. We would never have to worry of thirst again.

I looked at the old man. His eyes were wide with excitement.

He whispered loudly and snickered, "Have you ever seen anythin' more purtty in your entire life?"

I was about to answer but remembered the flickering campfire that rested across the cavern. There was a small shelter and several crates casting shadows on the opposite side of the wall. We weren't alone. I held my breath, wishing to atone for our brash entry into the cavern. I prayed that our silence meant something, but I couldn't believe not a single soul inside of that cave didn't hear us slurping down their precious treasure.

The light of the dancing flames shimmered across the open water as we slowly made our way towards the campsite. We didn't see a single soul as we drew near. Only vibrant shadows flickered against the walls. I gave a sigh of relief and made myself a silent promise never to be so stupid again. The two of us said nothing and listened to the soft crackling of the campfire flames. We drew our blasters, and our breathing was short and quiet. There was no one to be seen.

Walking past the campfire, I saw two small lizards being cooked rotisserie-style over the open flames. Surrounding the tent were crates of supplies. Glancing inside, I found solar panels along with a working generator. Looking inside another crate, I discovered medical supplies and a small collection of food rations.

The old man tapped my shoulder and pointed to the right side of the camp. Leaning against the rock was a corpse. The two of us approached the body. He couldn't have been older than forty. The putrid smell of his rotting body filled our noses. The old man gagged, quickly grabbed the edge of his gray hood, and covered his nose.

"What do you suppose did him in? You don't think it was the water, do yah?"

I shrugged and approached the body. In the dead man's hand rested his sidearm with his limp finger brushing the trigger. The horrid smell of the corpse became more pungent. Using the barrel of my blaster pistol, I searched for open wounds but found nothing. A spike of fear took hold of my heart. The life water we sought could very likely have been poison to our lips. I knelt, staring at the dead man and his lifeless cold eyes and should've panicked. I should've screamed with rage at the possible misfortune befallen us but didn't. Instead, I chuckled at the twisted irony of our fate.

"He wasn't shot or stabbed. He could've died from the water or natural causes."

The old man, frustrated, kicked at the ground. "That's just damn per-"

Suddenly, we heard noise from the tent. Startled, we pivoted towards the campsite, any worry about poison water shoved aside for this new threat. The old man took an angle, and I took the opposite side. Both of our weapons were drawn towards the tent's opening.

"Come on out!" hollered the old man. "We got yah surrounded! Our clan of fifteen men has the cliffside covered. Yah ain't goin' to escape!" A lie, but a good one. Would the tent's occupant call the old man's bluff? He continued, "If yah try anythin,' we'll shoot yah through, yah hear? Come on out of there with your hands held high!"

Two little feet poked out through the entryway of the tent. The shoes were small and worn. A child scooted out of the tent's opening and stood in front of us. She couldn't have been more than eleven years old. The young girl had long beautiful black hair and wore an oversized coat with a muggy shawl draped around her neck. Fear stained her soft blue eyes. Her small button nose was dripping, and her cheeks were smudged with dirt. She had a pair of thin small lips that were tightly closed as she looked anxiously upon us, awaiting our reactions.

"Well, I'll be damned," muttered the old man. His mouth was slightly ajar, and his sand-like eyes scanned her with bewilderment. He pointed to the body lying next to the wall. "Is that your pa?"

The little girl said nothing. Tears began streaming down her dirtied cheeks, making clean little rivers.

"How long yah been here?"

The little girl said nothing. She used her hand to wipe away her tears, smudging the dirt on her cheeks.

"Can yah speak?" The old man enunciated with his crispy dry lips, "Are-yah-deaf? Can-yah-read-lips?"

Still nothing.

I chuckled. "She can't read your scabbed lips, old man."

He became angry. "Damn it, girl! Who else knows yer here?"

She jolted with surprise but still said nothing.

"Well then, if my words don't work, maybe this language will." The old man lifted his blaster at the girl.

I aimed my pistol at the old man. "Put your gun down."

"If she ain't goin to tell us anythin', she's no use to us."

I pulled my trigger. The sound of my blaster echoed through the cavern. His body crashed to the ground. I holstered my pistol and looked at the little girl. She was shaking.

"Sorry you had to see that. Do you have a shovel?"

The little girl ran inside of her tent and pulled out a small trowel.

I sighed, "That will do."

It took time, but I drug the bodies outside of the cavern, through the tunnel, and heaved them over the cliff's edge. Below, I dug a crude grave at the base of the mountainside with the girl's small trowel. From time to time I would take a break and wipe the sweat off my brow and look up the cliffside. Sure enough, the little girl looked down upon me, watching as I proceeded with the burial.

I heaved their bodies into the open pit and heaped sand upon their lifeless forms. A gust of wind blew from behind me and aided me in covering their cold faces with the warm sand. Wind Mother and I finished the work, and the two of us sat next to the grave. I didn't say anything, but

Wind Mother gave the dead her final word and brushed the sand with her gentle hand. She drifted away without even saying goodbye.

I climbed back up the cliffside. The little girl handed me a small canteen filled with water from inside of the cavern. I looked at it cautiously, then back to her. She gave me a smile and a nod which I took as confirmation the water was safe to drink. My previous worries now buried, I gave my thanks, greedily drank the canteen empty, and followed her back through the tunnel.

She still hadn't spoken. We sat together around her campfire while she munched on her cooked lizards. I sat watching her, sipping on the water she gave me.

"You're probably wondering how we found you. I think you have the right to know."

She stopped eating and looked at me. I continued, "The old man said he'd heard about the spring from some people. I reckon he killed them, and he'd admitted as much. I'm assuming they were your kin?"

The girl sighed and took another bite of her lizard. A tear trickled down her cheek as she munched, but she quickly brushed it away.

I took another sip of water. "This planet's damn cruel. The people are, too. I'm sorry you must see such times."

The girl said nothing; she took a sip from her own canteen, ate another bite of lizard, and stared into the flames.

I chuckled. "It wasn't always like this, you know? This whole rock had water everywhere; a bit of green, too, if I recall the stories right."

The girl looked at me curiously.

I smirked. "Ah, you didn't know that?"

She shook her head.

I nodded. "Yup, the whole place was quite different long ago." I laughed and added, "Apparently, there was less sand."

She broke loose a smile, and I laughed. "Yes, indeed, those sure were different times. Probably filled with friendlier people, I would assume."

She handed me one of her half-eaten lizards, and I accepted. There wasn't much meat on the creature, but I finished it off, throwing its boney remains into the flames.

I stood up and threw dirt upon the fire. She gave me an angry scowl.

"You can't have fire like this going at night. People will be bound to see you, people far less kind than myself. Cook your food during the day."

I went to the spring, filled up my canteen and made my way towards the cavern exit. Through the tunnel, I found the familiar sandstone and emerged outside. The night sky was fading as dawn slowly breached the horizon. The bright morning sun crept from its hiding place and replaced the darkness with a hue of orange and red light that skimmed across the dunes of sand and vast planes, creating a sparkling glint across the desert landscape.

Suddenly, I felt a small hand reach out for mine. She was quiet; I hadn't heard her approach. I withdrew my hand quickly and looked down upon her. She gave me a longing look of sadness. She wanted me to stay.

"You can't come with me, girl. I'm no mother. I can't help you."

She pointed towards the desert. The morning wind was gently pushing the sand across the desert plane. I let out a deep sigh. "That's Wind Mother. She takes care of me. And now she'll take care of you."

I looked back down at her and something happened to me. Something I didn't expect. It was as if I was staring at new terrain. It felt similar to riding the endless waves of red sand dunes and suddenly entering into another plane of flat beige landscape; the change of atmosphere was a relief, a break from the monotonous ups and downs of the red slopes. A tingling sensation crept down my neck as if sand was trickling down my spine. I stared into her eyes and felt a warmth greet me, a heat unlike any sunrise had ever given me before.

Dread entered my heart. Not because of her pure and innocent gaze, but because for the first time in a long time, I was afraid.

For the first time in a long time, I suddenly cared. I had something to lose.

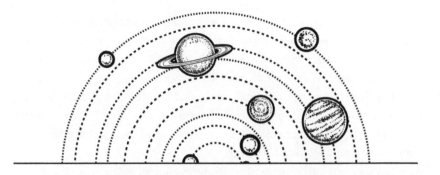

In the Image of the Gods

By Zachary Sherman

R andall blew a ring of smoke into the sky and watched as the currents of air ushered the tendrils of gray away. They vanished into the autumnal night sky as though they never existed.

"Don't you worry, I'll make more of ya'," Randall said. True to his word, he blew out ring after ring of smoke. There was little else to do; he had been waiting for hours in the parking lot for his commanding officer. "Good enough to drive him here, but not good enough to go into the facility with him," Randall muttered.

Truth be told, he was glad he hadn't been asked to go inside Ea Station. The stories he heard about it were enough to make his skin crawl. If even half of those stories were true...

"Then there's some busted up bullshit inside that concrete monstrosity," Randall murmured.

He tossed the cigar to the ground and stomped it out. He knew smoking one was pushing it; if he lit another, he would be spilling his guts into the toilet or on the side of the road before the night was out. At the same time, standing in the parking lot of Ea Station without anything to do but stare at the windowless, lightless structure made him feel queasier than smoking a dozen cigars could.

She had come from Ea Station.

He pushed the memory down by imagining his consciousness was a house, and below it, there was a basement—no—a dungeon. He put the memory of the woman back in its corner of the underground and locked the door to the cell, then all the doors in between.

His shaking hands fumbled with the lighter. He lit another cigar.

Within seconds, Commander Berkin stalked out of the facility. Randall opened the door to the back of the car for him, and the commander got in without saying a word to his driver.

Randall got in the car and started the engine. In the rearview mirror, Berkin's face glowered. The man was only fifty-nine but looked twenty years older tonight. Black circles danced beneath his eyes, almost tauntingly. His brow creased in either worry or rage—Randall couldn't always tell the difference. He hoped it was rage. The thought of a man who had fought in the Mech War feeling worry made Randall's stomach churn—or maybe that was the second cigar?

"Where to, sir?" Randall asked.

"What?" Berkin's eyes flickered towards Randall as if noticing him for the first time. Whatever had happened inside Ea Station had scared the hell out of him.

Damn. *I don't need one more thing to worry about*, Randall thought. However, he kept his expression impassive. He didn't want Berkin scanning him—not now, of all times. If he did, the commander might discover what Randall kept in the basement of his memory. And if that happened...

"Take me home," Berkin commanded. His tone was sharp, forceful. That was good. That meant whatever had occurred inside the station hadn't shaken his spirits too much. Perhaps there wasn't anything to worry about, after all. Perhaps Randall was just letting his imagination run away from him.

"Very good, sir," Randall said.

The ride would only take twenty minutes, and Randall expected the time to pass silently. Berkin typically read briefs or memos or simply brooded about his work. He would speak to Randall on occasion, but only in a professional capacity. To Berkin, Randall was a soldier; his place was to follow orders, nothing more. That was why Randall was surprised when the commander addressed him.

"How long have you worked for me, Randall?" Berkin asked. "I believe it's been twelve years."

"Seventeen," Randall said.

"Ah..."

Randall wondered if that was all the commander had wanted to say. The man was staring out the window of the car, almost listlessly, then said, "Did you serve in the war?"

"No, sir."

"Pity. The war built us. It gave us character. It gave us purpose. I do not believe there can be heroes apart from war—not because others lack sacrifice or pure intention—but because they lack a sense of duty and honor only war can engender." Berkin held a finger up purposefully. "War is the crucible that burns away soot and—once the smoke clears—leaves a nation with diamonds. No, more than that, war is the cradle of civilization. It can take a ragtag group of Bedouins and turn them into a nation, a people. It nurtures us."

"Is that a metaphor, sir?" Randall asked. He didn't like this talk of heroes and diamonds and nations. He barely liked chauffeuring a military man, let alone anointing the field of battle with holy water.

"Is that supposed to be a joke?" Berkin growled.

Randall's breath caught. *You idiot!* If he jerked Berkin around, the man might scan him out of spite, and then where would he be?

"No, sir," Randall said. "Just trying to understand."

Berkin snorted but didn't push the matter. He rubbed the leather seat next to him absent-mindedly and grabbed a bottle from the mini-bar in the back of the car. "I'm a goddamn commander in the mechanized infantry. They think they can throw me in a posh tin can with bottles of booze at my fingertips and expect me to keep quiet."

Randall didn't recall the commander minding the free chauffeur service and its complimentary bar in the past. Perhaps the man had borne the burden in silent suffering for the past seventeen years, Randall thought dryly.

He didn't mind Berkin, not really. The man worked hard and seemed to serve his country well. Randall, for his part, did his job just fine. He drove Berkin to work in the morning, and got to read while Berkin sat in nigh-endless meetings all day. Then he drove Berkin home at night. Occasionally, there would be the odd deviation from the normal routine—like tonight had been. Even that wasn't too taxing.

"They expect me to stay quiet, but how can I?" Berkin mumbled, this time entirely to himself.

"Quiet about what, sir?" Randall asked. Berkin had never seemed this distraught before, and he certainly hadn't been willing to discuss anything sensitive with Randall in the past. What changed?

Berkin sighed, "Times are changing. That's what happens when you get a crop of young smart-asses running things. They don't know what it's like. How could they?" Berkin directed his gaze at the rear-view mirror and locked eyes with Randall. It was strange, but at that moment, time seemed to slow for Randall. He felt like he could hear the blood pumping in his veins, and the world lost part of its pull on him. He was floating up and away from reality, no longer bound by gravity or tragedy, but buoyed by something strange and bright.

What the hell just happened to me?

Then the moment was gone. Randall barely believed it, but the trip was over. He had somehow driven all the way to Commander Berkin's house and couldn't remember having done so. How had he lost so much time? He hadn't been drinking, he knew he hadn't.

"Thank you, Randall," Commander Berkin said, letting himself out of the car.

"Of course," Randall muttered, still in a daze.

The commander paused and glanced back at Randall. "You've been a loyal employee, Randall. I value the twelve years you've worked for me."

"Thank you, sir," Randall said. With that, Commander Berkin closed the car door and headed to his house. Randall chose to gloss over how Berkin had, once again, misstated the number of years they had known each other. It was enough to focus on the fact the man had complimented him. Receiving a compliment from Berkin was rarer than winning the lottery.

As Randall pulled away, he had no way of knowing those words of affirmation were the last compliment Commander Berkin would ever give to anyone.

As soon as he got home, Randall collapsed in exhaustion on the couch. He woke hours later to the smell of brewing coffee wafting from the kitchen like a beckoning campfire, inviting him to come near and warm his weary bones.

The woman was awake.

Randall groaned and stretched. He checked his communicator and instantly, his blood turned to ice. Commander Berkin was dead.

"You want any eggs?" she asked and stopped abruptly at the threshold between the kitchen and the living room. Randall wondered if she could see the fear etched onto his features like carvings into wood.

The woman put her hands on her hips and stared deep into Randall's eyes. As unimposing as she was physically, the woman had the capacity to seem larger than life through the way she used her eyes. They were like a physician's scalpel, carefully slicing through reality and parting the disease of falsehood from the truth. Her ability to see and *know* frightened Randall more than tanks or mechs ever could.

"What happened?" she asked.

Randall gulped back a lump of fear. He tried not to tell the woman much—it had been that way for weeks. The only problem was, there was no one else to tell.

"Commander Berkin was found hanged in his home last night. I've been asked to report to the Fifth Precinct for questioning."

"They suspect foul play?" she asked and took a seat beside Randall.

He didn't like it when she was too close to him. She smelled... wrong. It wasn't that she smelled bad, not precisely. But her body odor was distinct from anyone else he had met. He hadn't noticed it at first—why would he? —but knowing what she was, those small deviations were almost overwhelming to his senses; they screamed her wrongness.

"They didn't say. The man was aging, single. Could have been suicide," Randall said, but the words sounded hollow to his ears.

The woman shook her head, her tangle of hair sliding from side to side. She was like a wild thing; her hair was the color of deep hickory and matted like leaves on a forest floor. Randall made a mental note to buy the woman a brush. She shouldn't have to live like this.

Then again, she shouldn't be alive at all.

"You don't believe for a second it was suicide," she said. "What do you think really happened?"

Randall hesitated. Ever since she had shown up at his home, his world had changed. She had been hurt, but insisted that he not take her to the hospital. Then, when he dressed her wound, he quickly realized why that had been the case.

Her blood was the wrong color.

Randall should have reported her right there and then—he could hardly believe he had kept the secret for twenty-three days as it was! —but something stopped him. She had told him her name and said thank you. He couldn't turn in someone who was kind, someone who had a name. He tried to only think of her as 'the woman,' but in the back of his mind, her name drifted through his psyche.

Evita.

He suspected Evita was from Ea Station. She was probably one of the experiments they purportedly labored over in their lab—a Frankenstein come to life. Or she could have been one of the leftover monsters from the Mech War, captured and held for study, or instead of being terminated, simply out of compassion at Ea Station. Then again, did they do anything out of compassion?

"It doesn't matter what I think," Randall said. "As soon as I report to the precinct, they will scan me. Once that happens, both our lives are over."

Evita bit her bottom lip pensively. "I'm sorry I put you in this position."

Randall shrugged. "You didn't know. It was the perfect storm: you showed up here, Berkin was killed, and now—"

"You can't let them scan you," the woman said, cutting Randall off.

He snorted at the words. "What can I do to stop it?"

She stood and started to pace. Randall's living room was small—in many ways, his life was small—but she filled the space like an ill omen. Randall knew that whatever the woman asked of him would likely mean his imprisonment, if not his death. So why was he leaning forward to hear what she would say next?

"I didn't ask this before because I didn't want to put you in danger, but given the circumstances..." The woman took a deep breath and stopped pacing. "I want you to go to Ea Station with me."

"What?" Randall was on his feet in a flash. Had she really just asked him to walk into the proverbial lion's den? Ea Station was off limits to everyone. Even Berkin himself required an invitation to enter the labs on the bottom floor—something Randall had heard him grumble about on more than one occasion.

"We have nothing to lose and everything to gain," Evita pleaded.

"Jesus Christ," Randall muttered. "If we're going to do something reckless, I say we get in the car and drive east until we're out of fuel." *We?* Since when did he think of him and Evita as a 'we'?

The woman shook her head. "They'd catch us. I know some of what is in Ea Station—the secrets the military would do anything, give anything, to keep out of the public's knowledge. It's the leverage we need to stay out of prison and off the chopping block."

Randall sank back onto the couch and put his head in his hands. He could go to the precinct and get sent to jail for harboring a fugitive or he could go to the station with Evita and risk being blown to smithereens by the guards. Given that one of those was a death sentence, the choice seemed simple: he would go to the police.

But what about her?

Randall looked up at Evita. She had disrupted his life, yes, but she had added to it as well. He enjoyed his conversations with her over the past few weeks and enjoyed waking up to the smell of coffee each morning and to the sight of her. He wasn't certain, but he thought he may have grown to love her. Wasn't that strange? She was a monster—grown from a test tube—and yet she was more human to him than most of the people in his life.

The pitiful excuse for a life I have, he thought bitterly.

An ember deep inside his soul was fanned into flame. He had spent his whole life hiding, he knew that was true. He had been a chauffeur for most of it, driving Berkin or other importants like him around, but *he* had never been important. He had never done anything that mattered. The thought of going on adventure, of doing something that mattered for a change, was intoxicating to him. If his options were going to prison until he grew old or doing one spectacular thing at Ea Station, why the hell not go for the spectacular?

"Fine. I'm in," he said.

Instantly, Evita's face brightened like the sun breaking through a cloudy horizon. Randall felt a pang in his chest, not entirely unpleasant. At that moment, he knew he would die for her and worried this realization would soon be put to the test.

Randall parked a good half a mile away from Ea Station; he didn't want them to see the headlights. They walked the rest of the way. The air was brisk on his face, making his cheeks flush and his eyes water. He had never felt so alive... or so close to death. He checked to make sure his gun was safely tucked into the waistband of his pants.

Evita fiddled with some sort of device as they approached the door. It resembled a walkie-talkie.

"What is that?" Randall asked.

"It will block the cameras. Best not to be seen," she said,

The front door was a large concrete slab on massive hinges. Randall imagined ramming a tank into it might not break it. Another part of him wondered if the door was there to keep unwanted intruders at bay or to keep the monstrosities within the lab contained.

Probably a little bit of both.

The door had a four-digit code, and Randall looked to Evita expectantly. She shrugged. "I don't know it."

"You had us come all the way here and you don't know how to get inside?" Randall hissed.

"I thought you might know. After all, you served with Commander Berkin for years, and I know he came here annually, at the very least."

"Yeah, but he was tight-lipped. Our relationship was purely professional. He forgot how many years I had served him last night... twice."

A memory hit Randall like a lightning bolt. Berkin rarely made mistakes, especially when it came to data. There was no way in hell he would have mixed up the number of years Randall had worked for him. He had been trying to tell him something. Maybe he had known he might die that night.

"What is it?" Evita asked, noticing the expression on Randall's face shift.

"He said I had served him for *twelve* years. That may have been a hint," Randall said.

"What's twelve times three hundred and sixty-five?" Evita asked.

"Four thousand three hundred and eighty," Randall said, barely thinking about it. She should have been able to do simple math herself.

Randall plugged the number into the keypad: 4-3-8-0. Instantly, a red throbbing light lit up the screen. A warning ran across the surface of the keypad. It told Randall he had fifteen seconds to input the right code or else security would be called."

"Shit!" He cried.

"Leap years, leap years!" Evita hissed.

Randall plugged in the numbers: 4-3-8-3. Instantly, the keypad flashed green, and the door unlocked.

Evita whooped in delight and headed inside, but Randall hesitated.

"What's wrong?" She asked.

"How could he have known I would figure it out?" Randall asked. "I'm just a chauffeur."

"Maybe the message wasn't for you? Berkin might have left it for whoever scanned you."

Randall grunted in reply. Whatever the reason, they didn't have time to waste pondering it. He followed Evita into the facility. As the door sealed behind him, part of him wondered if his fate had just been sealed as well.

Evita led him through the dizzying array of hallways at a brisk pace. They descended deep into the structure. Like Theseus following the golden thread out of the labyrinth, only they were plunging *into* the labyrinth; the concrete bones that held it together had chips, scrapes, and—in one place—even claw marks on them. They passed sealed doors with signs that said, "Warning: Keep Out" "Dangerous Specimen," or had radiation symbols plastered on them. Randall shuddered at the thought that somewhere there might be a switch that could open all those doors, unleashing a Pandora's Box of horrors on the world.

It wasn't long before they came to Evita's destination. This door, unlike the others, was entirely unmarked. There was no danger sign and no warning symbols, yet Randall was sure this was where Evita had originated. Not for the first time, Randall wondered if he could even trust her.

But his life was over anyways, no matter what he did. Might as well make it interesting.

Evita opened the door. Randall followed her in and was surprised to see that the room was nothing like a lab. There were no beakers, operating tables, or sterile, whitewashed walls. Instead, the interior of the room was spacious and cozy. The walls were a warm, inviting shade of lilac, and floral prints adorned the space. Sofas, tables, chairs, and recreational equipment lined the room. Multiple doors led to other chambers where Randall assumed sleeping quarters lay.

As for the inhabitants of the room, they were human—or, at least, they looked human. There were about a dozen of them, and they gaped at Randall and Evita as they entered.

Evita took off her shoe and propped it in the threshold of the doorway, so it wouldn't close behind them. Then she ran to the people in the room, hugging them one-by-one and flashing a relieved smile into their midst.

"You brought one of *them* with you!" One of the men in the group exclaimed. He was young, tall, fit. The others allowed him the place of prominence in their group as if it was second nature.

"Let me guess, if she's Eve then you're Adam?" Randall said dryly. He gestured to the man and wondered if they were the building blocks for some kind of new species.

"My name's Desmond," the man spat.

"I had to bring him," Evita said, ignoring their exchange. "There was no other way for me to get in by myself. He's fine, Desmond. Don't worry about it."

"Don't worry about it? They're dangerous. We should destroy it," he gestured to Randall.

Randall stiffened. *Is this the thanks I get?* Part of him thought about kicking the shoe out from the door's threshold and leaving them all to their fate. But he had made a promise to Evita, and he wasn't about to leave her.

"Don't call Randall an *it*," Evita said. "He's my friend."

"You can't be friends with them," Desmond growled.

"Too right you are," an unfamiliar voice sounded outside the compound's door.

Randall jumped at the noise and whirled around. Before he could even make out who was behind him, a fist slammed into his stomach. He doubled over, wheezing in pain. Then his assailant pushed him hard in the chest, sending Randall staggering backwards into the room with Evita and her people.

Randall straightened to see an old man in a lab coat, glaring at him. The man snatched up Evita's shoe and stepped into the room. Instantly, the door closed and locked.

"No!' Evita cried.

The scientist looked like he was ancient but moved with the grace of a fawn. Randall couldn't quite understand it. The man shouldn't have been able to hit him so hard or move so fast.

"I thought I would have to send a battalion to retrieve you. Instead, you returned to me on your own. That was very considerate of you, Number Four," the scientist said.

"It's Evita," she said through gritted teeth.

"You must have known I would be watching. To enlist the aid of one of our own..." The scientist glanced at Randall, almost dismissively. "How did you turn him? Did you rewrite his code?"

Code? What was he walking about?

"He helped me because he wanted to. I didn't force him. I'm not like you," Evita spat.

The scientist turned back to Randall, more interested this time. "Tell me, is that true? You were not coerced into assisting her, but chose to do so? That is unprecedented. I would love to get you on my table; take you apart and see what makes you so different from the others."

Randall took a step back from the scientist—the man was fast despite his age. He wanted as much distance between the two of them as possible. He felt for the gun in his waistband and pulled it out, pointing the weapon at the scientist's head. "Not happening. Instead, you're going to let us go."

The scientist cackled. His expression was one of vague amusement, and he didn't seem worried in the slightest. His cavalier attitude fueled Randall's rage. He was starting to think putting a bullet in the man and being done with it might be the best course of action.

"I order you to lower the gun," the scientist said.

"No," Randall replied.

This time, genuine surprise and concern flickered across the scientist's face. "You disobeyed me. You weren't programmed to do that."

"Programmed?" Something in Randall's head sounded like a claxon. His knees felt weak, he had the strongest urge to lay down and sleep, but he fought it off.

"He doesn't know what he is," Evita cried. "Just let us go. We'll take Randall with us."

"Like hell we will!" Desmond exclaimed, "I don't want any filthy Synth coming with us."

Synth? "What are you talking about?" Randall screamed. "I'm the one with the gun, so everyone better listen up and answer *my* questions. What is this Synth business? What are all of you? You're not human, I know that. I saw her blood," Randall gestured to Evita.

Evita sighed. "You're wrong, Randall. I'm human, but you... you aren't."

"What? That's ridiculous."

"It's part of your programming," Evita explained. "We made sentient robots as workers, spies, and soldiers. After the Mech War, something went wrong. You became confused."

The scientist chuckled. "Confused is an understatement. They became schizophrenic. You, Randall, and your robot pals had been made to appear so human you convinced yourselves you *were* human. You rounded up the original inhabitants of the world and put most of the homo sapiens to death. Destroyed by the ones they created, like the Titans of old falling to the gods of Olympus. Or the gods of Olympus falling to the overly rational minds of the enlightenment. One thing in history stays true, people always kill their gods."

"That can't be," Randall murmured. *Go to sleep, go to sleep, go to sleep,* his mind screamed. He was tired, so very tired all of the sudden, as if a veil was lowering across his mind. Maybe he should close his eyes—

"Randall!" Evita snapped, jolting him back to the present. "Your programming dictates that you shut down if you find out the truth. You need to fight it. It was supposed to be a failsafe, so the Synths wouldn't establish an identity apart from humanity."

"Instead, they established an identity *as* humanity," the scientist said. "I am most pleased my creators did not hide such an insidious Trojan Horse within me. There are advantages to being an older model: I don't age, I don't confuse fiction with reality, and—unlike Commander Berkin—I don't commit suicide when I learn an inconvenient truth."

"You told Berkin?" Randall asked.

"Yes," the scientist sighed. "I needed him to recapture Evita and thought he could bear the weight of the truth. A pity he could not. Ah well, so few can. You, however, are taking it quite well. What's your secret, Randall?"

"Shut up!" Randall screamed. The voices of Evita and the Scientist blurred with the clanging in his minds. The noise threatened to split his skull open. He had to stop that incessant noise, he had to.

He jabbed the barrel of the gun into his forearm.

"Randall, don't!" Evita screamed.

The bullet screamed from the barrel, tearing through Randall's flesh and bone. The proximity to his arm left a circle of burnt flesh around the entry point, and smoke rose both from the gun's barrel and his flesh. The bullet went straight through his arm. It came out the other side, splattering the ground with purple blood and fragments of...

"No," Randall whimpered. On the ground, in his own blood, were wires and chips. He looked at the hole in his arm. What he thought as blood was some kind of lubricant, moving through his systems. His skeleton was a reinforced plastic frame, designed to appear like bones. In the center of it all, wires, processors, and converters dictated his movement.

He was a machine.

Randall pointed the gun at Evita. "This is your fault!"

"None of the Synths have progressed this far," the scientist observed and leaned forward, fascinated, taking Randall apart with his eyes, down to the gears and wires and motors that were his heart, bones, and soul. The scientist's clinical detachment made Randall's blood boil—or whatever the hell it was running through his veins.

His thoughts raced. If he pulled the trigger, if he ended her and the other humans, none of this would need to be true. He could bind his wound, he could go back to his life. Surely, if everyone on Earth thought they were human, like Randall, then that must make it true.

"Killing me won't change what you are," Evita cautioned. Her eyes darted from Randall to the gun and back. She was trying to assess the situation, trying to manage it.

I'm tired of being managed.

Randall pulled the trigger.

Evita had known something like this might happen. She had thought about trying to rewrite Randall, but even with her superior technical skills, she didn't know where to start when it came to Synths. Instead, she had resolved to trust not in her technical expertise, but in Randall's humanity.

Her escape took years to plan. It had been precise, meticulous, foolproof—or so she thought. On her way out of the facility, she got tagged by one of the sentry lasers. If she had been half a second faster, she would have made it. As it was, she stumbled through the countryside, bleeding from a wound below her left rib and cursing her foolishness, until she made it to Randall's house.

She thought everything had gone to hell, that he would turn her in, even as she begged him not to. But he hadn't. Randall had taken care of her.

She tried to tell him what he was once, but he had shut down. The failsafe at work. She didn't bring it up and resolved to leave once she had regained her strength. She would never see him again, and she certainly couldn't risk going back to Ea Station alone. She would start a new life. Maybe find a pocket of humanity somewhere.

But there was one day, about a week before their trip to the facility, everything changed.

"I'm home," Randall said as he strode into the house.

"You're early," Evita observed. "Dinner's almost ready. This time you won't have to reheat it."

Synths didn't need to eat, but they had convinced themselves they did. They didn't need to sleep, but they shut down at night. They didn't need to age, but their bodies changed, anyway. It was as if they wanted the frailties of humanity and collectively willed it to happen. Evita couldn't hazard a guess as to why.

She caught Randall staring at her as she moved around the kitchen. She couldn't risk leaving the house—after all, Ea Station was certainly looking for her—and cooking was one thing she did to feel useful. Whether mechanical or culinary, she had always been good at combining components and crafting something new. Still, she was eager to stop playing housekeeper for a robot and get on the road.

"What is it?" Evita demanded. She didn't like how Randall looked at her. It was a hungry look—and not because dinner was almost ready.

"You're kind," Randall said.

Evita blinked in surprise. "Oh, uh, thank you. Was there anything else?"

Randall shrugged. "I didn't expect a monster—sorry—a mutant to be able to be kind. Is mutant okay to say?"

"Both monster and mutant are offensive," Evita snapped. *Besides, you're the monster, not me.*

"Do you want a cigar?" Randall asked.

"No. I don't think you should smoke inside; it isn't good for your health or mine."

Randall shrugged, lighting the cigar. "We're all going to die eventually."

But you don't have to, Evita thought bitterly. The Synths played human, living and dying like them, but it was all so senseless. They didn't *need* to live this way.

Randall exhaled, and the smoke hung heavy in the air. It had wormed its way into the walls over the years, and the room was stale with it. Evita wondered how something so temporary could leave such a lasting stench.

"Are there others like you?" Randall asked.

Evita hesitated. Most of the humans had been culled by the Synths, but there were pockets of humanity in the world. And there were her friends in Ea Station. They had been imprisoned by a robot she knew only as the Scientist. He seemed to know what he was, and he kept the humans alive for, what he liked to call, 'humanitarian reasons.' However, Evita was certain there was more to it than that. The Scientist had a purpose for them; she just didn't know what it was.

"If they're anything like you, then I'm sorry they're stuck in there," Randall said. He inhaled a bit too deeply and coughed on the smoke.

Just like a human would.

———————

The bullet whizzed past Evita's head, burying itself in the wall behind her. She felt her body collapse like an accordion with relief.

Randall sank to the ground and placed his free hand to his forehead. "I'm sorry, I'm sorry," he stammered. He rocked back and forth like a child for a few seconds. Then, he stopped moving entirely.

The room went still, and energy rippled through the air like a current. Evita and the Scientist looked at the gun and then locked eyes.

Evita ran for the gun, her legs moving like pistons beneath her, but the Scientist was faster. He reached to take the gun from Randall's hand, and Evita knew it was over for them.

A shot rang out. The Scientist stumbled backwards, eyes wide in surprise. Orange fluid oozed from the fresh hole in his chest, and a wisp of smoke floated from the barrel of the gun.

The gun Randall had fired.

"You don't understand. They're not—" the Scientist stammered out, but Randall didn't let him finish. He rose to his feet and unloaded the remaining three bullets into the Scientist. The sound of scraping metal and sparking wires sounded through the room. The robot that was the Scientist tumbled lifelessly to the ground.

Randall threw the gun to the ground and considered Evita and the other humans.

She wondered if he would take their lives next. Had they pushed him too far? Was he operating on instinct and impulse at this point?

Randall took a cigar, lit it, and offered it to Evita. She shook her head, refusing to take it. He grunted and shoved the cigar between his teeth. Leaned against the wall wearily, he gestured to the Scientist's body. "I think there's a key on his belt. You should take it and go. Someone might have heard the shots."

"What about you?" Evita asked.

"I'm going to wait for them. I'm going to let them scan me," Randall said. His jaw was set, his eyes determined.

"They'll learn everything. They'll know that you helped me, that you killed the Scientist, that you let us go. They'll kill you for it."

Randall nodded. "Probably. But once my memories are uploaded— once they scan me—they'll learn the truth. If their failsafe's trigger, they'll shut down. If they learn to resist, like I did, then they'll start new lives. Whether I survive and carry the message on, or the ones who scan me do it, the truth will spread like fire."

"What you're talking about...It's genocide. Some of your people will shut down. They'll die," Evita said.

"Yes. But those who survive will lead lives no longer built on lies. They will live to the fullest as what they were made to be: Synths."

"You could come with us?" Evita offered.

Randall shook his head. "The best thing I could do for you and the other humans is stay here. Once they scan me, no matter how it plays out, things will change. The world will be a safer place for you, a better place."

"Why would you do this? You're a Synth, not a human," Desmond demanded but his expression had softened, and the hate drained from his eyes.

Randall blew a ring of smoke into the air. It hung there for a moment, and Evita watched as the tendrils of smoke clawed towards heaven, desperate to survive. Then they slowly dissipated; in seconds, it was as if they had never existed.

"We should go," Evita said. She kissed Randall on the cheek, and led her ragtag band of humans to the surface.

They ran through the halls, constantly looking over their shoulders for fear of pursuit. None came—the first bit of luck they'd had yet.

Once they reached the top, Evita fell to her knees on the concrete, breathing in the crisp night air. It was like fire in her lungs, stoking a furnace of potential. It was good to be alive, to be free.

As she knelt taking in deep breaths, her had a crazy idea. What if this had happened before? What if she and her fellow humans were less—or more—than they thought they were? Part of her wished she had a knife to reveal her own inner workings like Randall had done, just to make sure she was truly, fully human.

She shook the idea off as she rose to her feet and beckoned for the others to follow her. After all, it was crazy. She knew she was human. She knew her own mind. She had seen her own blood, and it was the correct color, an emblem of her humanity.

Her blood was green.

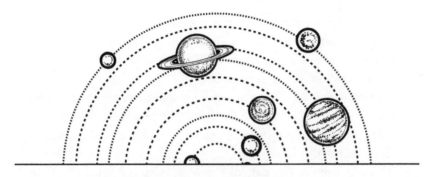

The Last Echo

by Rick Cooley

T he *Velocity Echo, United States exploration vessel. Crew....586. Year of launch....3078. Current status....Missing.*

The ship's computer relayed the status report to Captain Harlan Wescott and his bridge crew.

When they first encountered *Echo*, the initial perception was she was a Martian mining ship, but because of the sheer size and the fact she was suspiciously unaccompanied, Harlan ordered a quick scan out of curiosity. Such a scan was initiated on a regular basis. Consequently, there was rarely an issue to resolve. The area was policed by Martian Safeguard Space, a defense initiative that meant keeping traffic under close monitoring.

When the status report revealed the *Velocity Echo* had last made contact with Earth 976 years ago, there was considerable shock amongst the bridge crew. Harlan had the ship scanned three times before eventually, although still skeptically, believing the reader.

"Where the hell have you been?" Harlan whispered to the ship, looking at it through the huge window from his seat on the bridge. He swiveled his chair to face his coms team. They were listening for signals, radio messages, or mayday beacons.

"Can we get them on the radio?" he asked with a hint of excitement. Was it conceivable they were looking at a ship close to a millennia in age?

As they edged closer, he started to believe it. First, his scanner was never wrong. Second, and more significant, despite the darkness, as the light from their own ship gradually hit the hull of the *Velocity Echo*, its archaic architecture slowly became clear.

"I'm getting nothing, Captain" was the response from his chief operator.

Harlan stood in silence with the rest of the bridge as they listened to the crackling radio, waiting for a response. Harlan eventually pressed the mic button himself.

"This is Captain Wescott of the Mars Cruiser Taurus 5. Please respond, over."

There was silence, nothing.

"If I may, sir?" Lieutenant Clavell interrupted. "If that ship is as old as we are being informed—well—are we really expecting a response? After all this time?"

He was saying what they were all thinking, Harlan concluded, looking thoughtfully at his Lieutenant.

"Do you suggest we don't bother trying, Lieutenant?"

If Harlan was angry or embarrassed, he didn't show it. He did, however, concede all attempts at contact would likely be futile. He looked at his bridge crew standing away from their seats looking at the *Velocity Echo* through the massive observation window. The ghostly sight of the blacked out ship was made all the more eerie by the sound of undisturbed radio crackling around them.

The decision to board *Velocity* was approved by Mars command who advised caution at the discovery. Forensic science teams were dispatched and were en route, but they would take a day or two. Taurus 5 was given permission to send a reconnaissance team to the ship and check its safety before the scientists arrived. As a part of the Piracy Intervention Fleet (PIF), Taurus 5 was equipped for intercepting and boarding hostile ships. As such, highly trained boarding teams and the tools they required for breaching vessels were available to Harlan.

The likelihood of aggression appeared to be slim, and a small team with one shuttle was picked for the operation. No chances were being taken, and the armory was relieved of a selection of its assault weapons and tactical entry equipment.

Harlan decided he would personally join the team on the shuttle. It was unusual for a PIF Captain to personally board another vessel, but he had every intention of seeing the inside of the *Velocity* for himself. He hadn't, however, told Mars Command his intentions. Technically, no orders were being disobeyed.

On his way to the launch bay, Harlan headed down the decks to see his chief science advisor, Dr. Jess Brady. News of the discovery had spread to the rest of the ship, and Jess herself was desperate to be amongst the first to explore the *Velocity*. When Harlan reached the lab she was sitting by her computer, researching old Earth-made ships.

"I take it you're aware of the situation, Dr. Brady?"

"Absolutely. Take a look at this." She spun the monitor screen to face Harlan. "*Velocity Echo* was registered missing in 3083."

Harlan looked at the ship on the screen, then took a comparison glance at the *Velocity* out of the science lab window.

It was the same ship.

"Where do you suppose it's been?" he asked her.

"I have some theories I could share now or whilst aboard the shuttle. I take it you're here to recruit me for the landing party?'

"Correct."

She hurriedly gathered her things and followed behind Harlan, who, not for the want of politeness, was heading towards the shuttle bays.

On board the shuttle, Harlan briefed the six-person landing team with the aid of Jess. Unlike the highly trained soldiers strapped into their seats in front of her, she hoped to extract and examine artefacts from within the waiting relic.

"We've been unable to communicate with *Velocity Echo* and are authorized to explore before the scientists take over. We will be on our guard, but I expect this to be purely reconnaissance," Harlan said. He went over the different scenarios regarding airlock entry as well as the limited history of the ship and its potential layout. Once he'd finished, he nodded to Jess so that she could add her own brief.

Jess cleared her throat nervously. Despite the small number in front of her, she wasn't used to public speaking. "The ship is old, but I don't expect any issues with its integrity as degradation is unlikely. We won't know if there is oxygen until we assess the second internal airlock. I advise we stay fully suited regardless of the oxygen readings once inside." She regarded them from her seat. No one spoke. "Any questions?"

A hand casually raised from a young male private. Jess smiled and nodded towards him. "Yes, Private Bell?"

"What do you think we will find?"

Jess looked at Harlan before answering. "We have no idea, in all honesty. I would like to know what happened to it, and more importantly, find out why the hell it decided to show up now."

––––––––––––

The *Velocity* was in total darkness and was only visible due its current angle towards the sun. The stillness of it against the blackness of space made it all the more haunting.

Harlan's orders were to send in one team, but looking at it from the smallness of the shuttle, he was concerned it was too big a job for the eight of them. If Mars Command could have seen what he saw, they may have told him to hold off.

First impressions were no discernible external factors were the root cause of the *Velocity*'s missing status. If it had been in a fight, it certainly wasn't obvious. A flyby of the ship was enough proof no attack had taken place.

Upon landing, the integrity of the airlocks and docking bays confirmed nobody had broken in, which meant they would need to.

Manx and Davies loaded a charge to the dead airlock control panel. Once destroyed the mechanism to the outer airlock was released and they were manually able to open it. Lifeform scans flashed eight green dots, and the oxygen readout was good, so good that the idea of suits was abandoned.

Jess was immediately suspicious. There was no power and yet there was oxygen, by all accounts plenty of it. The elation at the abundant oxygen levels was evident on all of their faces, but she was duty bound to rain on their parade.

"I'm not sure that this ship is as old as we think," she said, looking puzzled.

"What makes you say that?" Harlan asked, surprised.

"With no power the oxygen filtration should have stopped. They had to have had power until recently."

The group was instantly uneasy.

"May I suggest extra caution in light of this possibility?" She looked concerned.

Not sure what further caution they could take, Harlan politely nodded.

Their suits were left in a pile by the final airlock, and they began to make their way through the labyrinth of corridors and stairwells. They navigated simply by the signs on the walls clearly marking the way, noticing that some of the emergency lighting on the ceiling and floor provided a faint red glow. It was welcome, but ultimately, they couldn't see anything without their headlamps.

Personal effects of the crew and the things they had discarded, now technically artifacts, lay in abundance in the rooms they passed. They looked for any clues as to what might have happened, but it wasn't until an hour or two of searching the lower three decks they found a member of the missing crew in the large gymnasium turned to sleeping quarters.

The body, obviously dead but not for that long, was a male of indeterminate age. He sat hunched against the wall surrounded by what appeared to be his own personal effects. His brown leathery and mummified body was still dressed in engineering overalls.

"He's been dead fifty or so years looking at the decomposition, but no planetary atmosphere may alter that a bit," Jess said, crouching to take a closer look. The others looked at her blankly. "There are no flies," she continued, "but he certainly isn't nine-hundred-years-old."

On his lap lay a note written in scrawled but legible handwriting.

O'Connor picked it up and read it aloud for the others.

"To the finder: I have lost track but think it to be 3109. We have been lost for around thirty-one-years. I've now locked them all on the engineering floor and above. Please understand they were mad and we had absolutely no choice. The four others that I escaped with have passed away. I have since released their bodies into space. To Mary, I love you, knowing I will never see you again and the extreme loneliness recently has driven me to this and for that I'm so sorry. Engineering Officer Herb Stillwell."

They looked at Herb, feeling sadness for him and his final days—years?—alone. The biggest question they had was not what was going on, but when had it started?

According to the information, the ship was nearly a thousand years old, but the interior suggested otherwise. The most likely theory was they

THE SENTIENT SPACE: IS THERE ANYONE OUT THERE?

had somehow travelled back in time to the ship as it was, perhaps a hundred years or so after it had gone missing.

Jess further mused that the only possible explanation was a wormhole, and they had travelled through one whilst on board the *Velocity*. Most likely, it was the same wormhole with which it had arrived.

Harlan's fears intensified when they were unable to get hold of the Taurus 5. He contacted the shuttle parked in the docking bay and asked for a report from Taurus 5.

"Captain, I can't see them at all," came the concerned voice of the pilot, Cole. "What's going on, Captain?"

"Did you notice anything, Cole? Did you see them leaving?"

"No, Cap. I'm so sorry. Things went blurry—I think I may have passed out."

"No need to apologize, Cole, but we might be in a real situation here. Dr. Brady thinks we may hit a wormhole. I'm going to need you to try and get help."

The Taurus was gone. With no way of transmitting a mayday aboard the *Echo*, Harlan sent Cole and the shuttle to see if it could pick up any singles from local traffic and call for help.

———————

The team looked disheartened, and Harlan wasn't sure if he could lift them. "Let's find out what's been going on," he said decisively.

"Do you suppose Herb turned the power off ?' Davies asked everyone as they left the gym. "Fifty years ago?" he added.

"It appears so," Jess replied.

"I think we should head up and see if we can get some power into this thing," Harlan said, a suggestion meant as an order.

Nobody said anything but the look on their faces said it all. The prospect of being lost in space proved to be a huge motivation killer. Most felt that waiting for Cole and possible help might be the best course of action, but pressed on despite fearing deep down there was no help coming.

The boarding crew followed the signs leading up to the engineering floor, which they felt was the most likely place to find the generators, but it was also the area Herb had warned them about.

The ship became more disheveled as they ascended. The floors appeared to have suffered from ransacking. They had to step over smashed internal windows, tables, cabinets, and doors. Some of the corridors were totally blocked and meant traversal through the damaged rooms, which was exceptionally tricky in the darkness. All tripped or fell more than once.

On the wall of the main stairwell to floor eighteen DO NOT ENTER was crudely written in red paint. The staircase was densely blocked with cupboards, doors, and wall panels. It took them a long while to clear a path, during which Harlan checked his radio. There was no word from Cole. The shuttle's departure added to the feeling of total isolation.

Floor eighteen was a mess. Before they had made the gap in the stairs, the air was thick and the smell putrid. The pollution caused a further problem as vision was impaired, the lamp lights less effective against the poor filtration. Thick floating partials danced around them.

A *blip* was picked up on the lifeforms scan.

"Oh my god," announced O'Connor.

They turned to look at her as she showed them her scanner. A small red dot flashed, indicating life a few hundred meters away, either on the same floor, above them, or below them. Despite the scanner's limited range, it was nonetheless accurate.

There was a brief discussion as to whether or not the thick air would affect its accuracy, but Harlan didn't need to give the weapons ready order.

Even Jess, ever the pacifist, readied her pulse pistol. They stood silently and waited. The dot didn't move initially for what felt like a long time, then suddenly streaked forward.

The team trained their guns and lamps along the dark, murky corridor to the far wall and the junction ahead. A small figure ran through the circles of light into the adjacent corridor.

"Holy shit!" three of them shouted, Harlan included. They stopped and waited. Moments later, the small figure appeared again, slowly this time.

"Christ, it's a kid," the tall veteran Manx said, more than a little surprised.

The boy's long matted hair fell down his filthy naked body. The team stood motionless at the sight. The boy turned to look into the light but quickly crouched and covered his eyes, the motion revealing sharp blackened teeth and long talon-like fingernails. He made a loud hiss towards them before scrambling away, this time on all fours. The team, dumbfounded, looked at the scanner before slowly pursuing.

"If there are children, then there are adults, right?" asked Bell.

"Must be," was the matter-of-fact response from Jess.

They rounded a corner and entered what was, according to the sign above the large double doors, the engineering hangar. It was massive. Their lights wouldn't reach from one side to the other.

Hanging from nine-foot pipework was a long row of bodies. They counted thirty-two adults, both male and female with the same naked feral appearance as the boy. The corpses were in different stages of decay, but it was clear none of the bodies had been there more than a few months.

The floor below the bodies was sticky with different layers of congealed blood likely from years of uncleaned spillage. Without a doubt, the worst thing was the smell, intensified to the point of becoming unbearable. After a few moments of retching, the team pulled gas masks from their kits. The visual impedance was preferable to the crippling stench.

Further exploration of the hangar uncovered a huge pile of bones and flesh, again in different layers and states of decomposition.

"What the fuck's going on her, doc?" Harlan asked, as the team's head-lamps searched.

"Cannibalism? It would explain the corpse pile." She pointed her pistol towards the hanging row of bodies. "I suspect that is their fluid source."

"Blood?" Harlan asked.

"Appears so. Blood is seventy-eight-percent water. They could in theory survive off the flesh and blood of the dead. I would suspect they are strung up alive, perhaps? I can't account for the haemochromatosis though."

"The what?" Harlan asked.

"Blood is iron-rich. In short, too much of it would be fatal," Jess said, panic starting to show. "My guess is that this is the original crew or its descendants, a hundred or so years worth of additions."

O'Connor's scanner blipped again. Two seconds later there was another.

An air vent door crashed open, and two adult males dropped into the path of headlights. They slowed as the light hit them, putting up their arms to protect their eyes so accustomed to the darkness.

More blips and more opening of air vents sounded.

"Halt!" shouted Manx at the two unarmed men slowly making their way towards him. He raised his gun but was not in the habit of shooting an unarmed assailant. Still, they came at them.

The sound of metal crashing against metal was unnerving but worse was their noises, a shrill screaming from multiple sources and difficult to pinpoint. The scanner continued to bleep but was overwhelmed by lifeforms.

"What the fuck do we do, Captain?" Manx, possibly, Davies shouted above the screaming.

Harlan didn't answer. Like rain, they fell from the hangar ceiling, landing on large crates and pipes to break the thirty-foot drop. The chaos of the team's lamps frantically searching looked like the stage lights at a rock concert. It was impossible to estimate the numbers. The screaming intensified and wasn't limited to the invading hoard.

There were gunshots. The team's pulse and laser rifles added to the dramatic light show. Someone landed on Harlan and knocked him to the ground. It was difficult to identify gender in the foggy darkness, but he thought it was a woman. Before she was able to pounce on top of him, he managed a kick. It landed on her chin, causing her to fall in pain.

With his rifle on the ground, he pulled his pistol from his waistband, just in time to shoot an assailant in the temple. Arms grabbed at him from all sides and he fiercely fought them off, blindly striking out in a circle.

His lamp light fell on O'Connor. She was being held from behind, her arms pinned. He was just in time to witness her throat be ripped open by the swift sweep of a long-fingered hand.

Fighting his way through unseen attackers and flailing arms, his light found Jess. Her pistol was gone, and she was wildly swinging a metal pole, the fear of being overpowered keeping her on her feet.

Harlan fired his pistol again and again. His shots hit their mark each time. He grabbed hold of Jess. "Let's get out of here."

The relief of not being alone woke up an inner rage, and she tore into the ranks of unarmed attackers with ferocity.

They scanned the blackened room looking for their comrades, shooting and hitting anything that strayed into their path. On the floor, Harlan could make out at least two motionless lights, most likely strapped to the heads of their fallen team. To get to them would be impossible.

Back to back, they made their way to the double doors, Harlan shooting one way and Jess swinging the other. Another moving light appeared. Jess recognized Bell, limping and shooting his way towards them. He made a signal as if to say keep moving but was hit on the back of the head with a thick iron bar. The whack knocked him to his knees. Like a locust swarm, the feral humanoids engulfed him.

Harlan and Jess ran down the corridor. The narrowness gave them a slight advantage. Despite the disgusting air, the light reflecting off of the walls improved their vision significantly. They were able to accurately pick off the chasing army behind them. The attackers thinned as they made their way through the eighteenth floor.

The odd stragglers pursuing them were dispatched quickly. Alone, they were pathetic, Jess was almost ashamed at killing such helpless prey.

They ducked into what appeared to be a control room with exit doors to the left and right. Happy they wouldn't be trapped, they barred the main door.

Harlan looked at her. "Are you all right?"

Stupid question.

"No, not really. I killed so many. They weren't even armed." She shivered with adrenaline.

"They weren't helpless. I think those claws count as weapons. They wiped out our entire team." Harlan was also clearly shaken by the ordeal.

"Now what?" She hoped he had an answer but knew there wasn't one. Not only were they trapped on a cannibal-infested ship, they had limited food and were likely lost in another time zone. It was one thing to escape the hangar, but what were they escaping to? If she was right, the world she knew wouldn't exist for hundreds of years. The thought made her sick.

"Let's get power turned on and head back to the gym," Harlan said with a sigh. "At least, Herb had food and drink."

The paneled wall bulged and buckled suddenly. Harlan immediately aimed his gun, but it gave way and flew at them with an unnatural force, knocking them to the floor and sending Harlan's pistol flying.

With a roar, a giant of a man burst into the room. He was scantily dressed in rags, a huge bloated belly bulging out of his ripped shirt. His height and bulk were as menacing as his rage.

Jess stumbled as the giant attacker grabbed a metal table and launched it towards her. She rolled away just in time. Harlan lay still, hopefully unconscious. The giant roared again and projectile vomited blood and guts from his mouth, painting the floor red with his diet of human blood and flesh.

Jess screamed in horror as he surged toward her. His clawed hand grabbed her by the throat and pushed her up against the wall, lifting her from the floor. He ripped Jess's lamp and mask from her head when it shone in his eyes. She was unable to scream but could smell his disgusting breath as he leant in to eat her face.

She heard a squelch and felt a warmness over her face. There was no pain as she fell to the floor next to the headless hulk.

Harlan held out his hand and pulled her to her feet. The next corridor led them to the generators. After working out a small and simple sequence of lever pulls, the ship burst to life. The lights momentarily blinded them. Screaming from the hangar suggested it had a similar effect on their attackers.

The noise of the ship springing to life lifted an emotional fog. For the first time since arriving on the ship, they felt positive, even if it was brief.

Exhausted, Harlan and Jess made it back to the fourth-floor landing. They collapsed and hugged each other for a long time.

Harlan approached the airlock corridor and was surprised to see the pile of suits were gone. Near the docking bay, he saw a fully lit room with a table and chairs. A half-finished bottle of whiskey sat on the top. In the corner of the room, an unrolled sleeping bag had seen better days. A computer screen blinked.

Harlan made his way to the monitor slowly and navigated to the log entries.

"Day 78. Today, I will finish the whisky. That will be my final act. Farewell."

He scrolled through more entries. One caught his eye. "Day 56. I woke up this morning to what I had dreaded the most. She is gone, and I am totally alone. I never told her I loved her, and now she will never know. After I figure out what to do with her body, I need to...."

Harlan stopped reading. His broken heart returned and hit him like a brick. He scrolled to the beginning of the log entries.

"Day 1. This is Captain Harlan Westcott of the Mars Cruiser Taurus 5. Amazingly, the ship had power. It turns out the emergency generators have never been used. Good news over, however. Only myself and Dr. Brady have made it through the madness. We have secured this floor by blocking all the doors and vents from the floors above.

"Taurus 5 is not in our vicinity. Dr. Brady thinks we passed through a wormhole whilst on *Velocity Echo*. This makes sense. Current dates from the ship computer are muddled. We don't know how long we will have food, water, or power. We will, however, find a way!"

Harlan looked down at his frail body and filthy clothes. The malnutrition was affecting his memories again. He had forgotten before, but unlike before, Jess had been there to remind him.

Harlan had loved her, and without her, he feared he was losing his mind. He glanced at the whisky bottle, wondering when exactly day 78 was.

Harlan was shaken awake. His eyes were foggy. The empty bottle of whisky fell from his side. Cole, the shuttle pilot, smiled above him. A group of strangers stood behind him.

"We're going home, Captain." Cole paused. "A new home, at least."

EPILOGUE

Dr. Jess Brady logged in to check her results. She was confident but relieved to see she had passed with honors in all areas. However, the excitement quickly left as she read further.

"Dr. Brady has demonstrated exemplary skill and would make a superb addition to the Mars Space Program. However, we are unable to grant her a post at this time."

Angry and confused, Jess called the agency but was told they had no further information. An hour later, she took an incoming video call. A 45-year-old man with a dark moustache appeared on the large screen.

"Dr. Brady, it's great to meet you. I am the Director of Human Intelligence for Mars' colonies," he began.

"Okay...I'm pleased to meet you," she greeted him with suspicion.

"I believe you were turned down for a role as a scientist within our space fleet. I am truly sorry about that, but I'm here to tell you, this has been an entirely purposeful decision."

"Go on," Jess replied curiously.

"Have you heard of the Echo Files, Dr. Brady?"

"No, should I have?"

"The Echo Files are an intelligence archive that began on Earth 800 years ago. They're a highly top secret set of documents guarded by trusted individuals and passed from generation to generation. The documents contain information of what is to come in the future, a set of very accurate predictions, if you like."

"Predictions? Are you telling me my career is being cancelled because I fucked up in the future?" she said, a degree of frustration in her voice.

He ignored the question. They were supposedly written by one man. Who he was and where he came from is not known, but he saw the future. Everything he predicted came to pass, and if there hadn't been any skepticism in the early days, thousands of lives may have been saved. He predicted wars, disasters and ultimately the exact date of Earth's end.

"Amongst the predictions was your birth and enrollment in the space agency. Of all the predictions, yours is the most specific. He instructed that you *never* be allowed in the program. There has been a great deal of debate around it for many years. It even has its own theories and writings based on it."

"This is crazy. Are you seriously suggesting that some ancient scripture is deciding my future?" Jess looked at his kind face and trusted him. It was so ridiculous she almost believed it. "What else can you tell me?"

"Like you, my birth was also predicted and as a result I was recruited to investigate you and take on this role." The director smiled. "I would like to offer you a position on my team."

She was intrigued. Her dream of space exploration was evidently over, and she had nothing to lose. "I need to know more, but—of course, I'm considering it, Mr—?"

"Wescott. Call me Harlan."

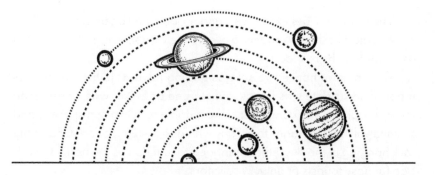

Any Port in a Storm

By Jay Mendell

When the proximity alarm went off in a series of irritating, high-pitched beeps, Zelkur knew his break was over. With a groan, the Dhaalgi staggered to his feet and stretched his back, letting his spine quills pop to release the last bit of tension.

Over a decade ago, the Whitcomb Company dropped a line his way, asking if he'd be interested in taking a position. Apparently, his credentials made him the perfect candidate. When he'd asked what credentials they were referring to, the representative hemmed and hawed before mumbling he had good problem-solving skills and a reputation for independent thinking, which meant he could sit and do his damn job without anyone hovering over his shoulder.

Zelkur had been job-free at that point, but retirement hadn't suited him. Working as the sole Attendant to Maverick Station on the far reaches of space, he was still retired, but had the added bonus of no one banging on his door trying to sell him life insurance.

It was a rare occasion he had to do more than sendoff automatically accumulated data and take stock of the fuel supply each month. Once in a while, he had odd repairs, but the station was largely self-fulfilling, with bi-monthly supply drops left by an unmanned ship, no contact required. It was a pretty easy position, all things considered.

There were always exceptions, and no job could be perfect.

The alert flashed. Wandering over to the view screen, Zelkur squinted as he studied the readouts.

Ah. An unauthorized vessel was drifting towards Jethro, the nearby moon. The satellite was left as undisturbed as Zelkur was, considering the atmosphere was completely inhospitable to all known species, and seemed willing and eager to kill any who dared step foot on it. For a big rock hanging in the sky, Jethro managed to function as the perfect death-trap for nosy tourists or unlucky solicitors.

Certainly, it wasn't his job to keep random interlopers from beating themselves to death against the moon's surface like a fly against the windowpane, but it was discouraged for anyone to die on your watch, regardless of how much they may have earned it.

Zelkur made his way to the communications board, flicking the rusty ON switch. "Unnamed vessel, this is Maverick Station. You are entering protected airspace. Please identify yourself."

There was a long moment of static, then a voice came in loud and clear. "Maverick Station? This is the Albatross! One-man scientific exploration vessel under the Malta Academy! My apologies for the trouble, I'm afraid my systems took a bit of a hit going through an asteroid field, and I've gotten myself quite turned around."

"Any immediate danger?" Zelkur said, frowning faintly as he prepared to let the vessel dock. If something happened to the Albatross's life-support system, he'd need to be ready.

"No sir!" the voice replied cheerfully. "Seems like the hit only took out navigations. Well, and my pride. But I have enough supplies to last me, if you wouldn't mind pointing me in the right direction."

"I can do ya one better," Zelkur rumbled. "Get on over here, I'll see what I can do to fix ya up."

"Oh? Oh! Thank you, sir. Setting the docking sequence now!"

Zelkur promptly cut the feed, letting the screen go dark.

Against all odds, it seemed that he was about to go do his job.

Maverick Station wasn't very big on its own but had enough room to allow people to gather inside, if not enough room for them to live there. The scientist aboard the Albatross, a Lauroo named Ikke, didn't seem to mind the cramped quarters as she cheerfully poked around, answering Zelkur's questions and asking a number of her own.

"And this garden is self-sustaining?" she asked, fascinated, as she studied the small pots set aside in a corner of the main room.

"Yup," Zelkur confirmed, unsurprised by her interest. Plants that could survive long-term in space, even within a ship's carefully controlled atmosphere, were rare. These species added consistency to his diet, since he was never certain what would show up in the supply drops.

Fixing her navigation systems was fairly simple—the equivalent to the old 'hit it until it plays dead' method that always served him pretty well. Ikke needed to wait for it to reboot, and she should be set.

"What kinda research are ya doing all the way out here?" he asked, mildly curious. The equipment on her ship was very specific, but nothing indicated she had a specialty in death planets or anything of the like.

Ikke beamed.

"Excellent question!" she chirped, her beak clacking excitedly. "I specialize in zoology, specifically creatures that are hard to track. I've published a number of papers on the subject. My current specimen of study is the Crax from Planet Yoldaet. Have you heard of them?"

"Can't say I have," Zelkur replied, bemusedly watching the way her feathers fluffed up.

"Well! They're two-foot quadrupeds with a startling tendency towards vanishing," she extolled, her vestigial wing nubs twitching in excitement. "A natural camouflage, I've found, rather than some of the more outlandish theories involving teleportation or the ability to induce hallucinations in the viewer. Entirely harmless, despite what some superstitions may claim. In fact, several of the plants you have on-board would fit in well with their dietary requirements!"

"Is that so?"

"It is!" Ikke nodded, impassioned. "I must commend whoever installed them, it's very professional work for the lack of space provided."

"Just me, I'm afraid," Zelkur said, a hint of a smile crossing his face. "I'm the only one onboard."

"Oh." She sounded a bit awkward. "You live here by yourself?"

"Indeed, I do," Zelkur confirmed and had to stifle a chuckle when her tail feathers drooped. He let out a sigh as he settled back down in his chair, letting his aching bones rest for a moment.

"Don't you ever get lonely?" Ikke asked, an honest curiosity in her voice. "I do a lot of solo work, but that's only for a few months at most, not years like your work. I have a lot of contact with other beings, even if they don't travel with me. I don't think I could imagine living out on the rim for decades without anyone else nearby."

Zelkur hummed considerably. *Was* he lonely? He didn't particularly think so. There were moments, of course, where he was hit by a sense of nostalgia for what his life had been and the people that inhabited it, but it was never bad enough to make him regret his decision. The work out here needed to be done, and Zelkur was in a unique position to fulfill it.

"This work ain't for everyone," he said slowly, trying to decide the best way to answer her question. "There used to be a lot more replacements, in the early days. Back when the stations were being set up, there were preliminary programs to try and outfit them. Eventually, they figured out how to make it work or found the right people. I'm one of them. So, no, I don't get lonely much. It suits me, being out here. I don't have many complaints."

"I see," Ikke mused. "I guess certain temperaments do adapt better to specific circumstances. It only makes sense that the Attendants would find ways to survive, if not thrive. It's a matter of adapting to the environment!"

Zelkur chuckled, tossing the spanner up and catching it in his opposite hand. "That sounds about right, Doc. I ain't no misanthrope—I like company just fine, and it's nice to see the folks that pass through. But I don't need it, y'know? It's another small bonus."

Ikke nodded thoughtfully. "Makes sense. Would you *want* a permanent companion, if you had one?"

Zelkur spun the spanner around a finger and glanced over the interior of the station around them. It wasn't exactly conducive to housing more than one person—they could squeeze in, sure, but Zelkur was certain there would be bickering over what space belonged to who, and use of the kitchen, and all that. Zelkur remembered the frustration from his Academy days—and didn't remember it fondly.

"Doesn't seem practical," he shrugged. "Maybe if I found somebody who suited the life, like I do. Even then, they'd have to content themselves with all my plants, 'cause I ain't getting rid of 'em."

Ikke laughed, raising a hand to block the sharp fangs protruding from her mouth. "And what a magnificent collection it is! It's the first thing I noticed when I walked in here."

"That's the point," Zelkur said, lifting his chin proudly. So many years of searching had to be worth something, after all.

"You have built something wonderful here, Zelkur," Ikke said, her eyes warm. Her beak was not exactly conducive for expressions like 'smiling,' but the intent was there. "Even if it wasn't on purpose, I'm very glad I got the chance to see something new."

Zelkur ducked his head, scratching at the back of his neck. "Well... I'm glad I got to see something new too, Doc."

―――――――――

His next encounter, several long months later, was not nearly so cheery. For as little as Zelkur received visitors, one would think he wasn't often held at gunpoint. This was incorrect, as only the desperate and the deranged were willing to travel to the edge of space, and both groups tended to be heavily armed.

Zelkur, with a gun to his head as he tended the wounded pirate, was mostly exasperated by the event.

"Gentlebeings, please! Our new friend cannot work when he is in distress!" Captain Enno cried out as he bled all over Zelkur's nice steel floors.

"He doesn't seem very distressed, Captain," said a large and menacing Fossnat. They were the only pirate who had managed to fit on the Station, but a number of dropships were hovering around, their communication feeds tuned in to what was happening inside.

"Why would I be distressed?" Zelkur said mildly. "We're friends, aren't we?"

"It's always good to make friends!" Enno said, enthusiastic despite the pained edge to his smile. "And a Station Attendant is a good friend to have!"

"So is a pirate," Zelkur returned, amused.

He finished passing the scanner over the pirate's body, and seeing nothing more of note, slapped a bandage into place before leveraged himself back up, ignoring Enno's hiss of pain.

"He'll be fine," he reported to the Fossnat, the closest thing the group had to a medic. "No risk of infection I can see, now that it's stopped bleeding. I'd say he's out of the danger zone."

They let out a strained sigh and bowed their heads to Zelkur. The gun was finally lowered, and Zelkur took it as a win.

"We owe you a debt," they said with a deep, rumbling voice.

Zelkur waved a hand, already dismissing it. "There's no debt between friends."

At that, the Fossnat let out an exasperated sigh, and Enno laughed wheezily from his place on the floor.

———————

Once the injured had been dealt with and their ship was refueled, the pirates were gone as quickly as they came. They hadn't paid for the fuel, but Zelkur was willing to cut his losses. There were far worse outcomes when dealing with a pirate ship, and lost fuel, no matter the monetary value, was worth less than his life.

That didn't mean he was left with no reward. However, it took him a few weeks before he realized it wasn't explicitly described as a 'reward', per say. After all, as Enno had loudly claimed, doing a favor for a friend was hardly something that needed thanks.

So, Zelkur took the increased supply routes to his lonely area of the galaxy with a grain of salt and pointedly did not ask where some of the new drop ships had *received* said supplies.

It didn't mean nobody asked—it took about a month and a half for a puttering old Space Patrol vessel to darken Zelkur's doorstep, an impressively fast time considering the usual rate of such things.

The sole officer on board, a Dreker who did not introduce himself, was tall and gangly, with long protruding limbs much like the rest of his species. With several extra arms and three pairs of eyes, there were plenty of opportunities for him to glare and cross his arms as he loomed over Zelkur suspiciously.

Zelkur did not appreciate it, though he understood the necessity. People who were small in spirit needed to appear big in stature—it soothed something deeply hurt inside their souls, and as always, Zelkur tried his best to accommodate for the needs of others.

"I haven't made any reports, sir," Zelkur repeated, keeping his thumb looped through his belt loop in order to prevent any temptation regarding what else he could do with it. "And I follow regulations, sir, by the book."

True enough. But if the regulations didn't explicitly state something, Zelkur found it was easier to come to his own conclusions.

"And you're *sure* no one has passed through here?" the Dreker asked, a touch of skepticism in his voice.

Zelkur merely shrugged, pointing to the flickering display at the nearest terminal. "The specifics are automatically recorded by the station when anyone passes by. Relative size of the ship, how fast they were going, all of it. Last one I had out here 'fore y'all was a little one-man exploration vessel that went off-course. I sent 'em on their way soon enough, but that's taken as a matter of policy. Yer welcome to take a copy of my records, sir."

The officer sighed and slipped his data pad back into his pocket. He could recognize a dead end when he saw one. "I'll take a copy, thanks. This is an official investigation, so I need to take necessary precautions."

"'Course, I understand," Zelkur nodded and meandered his way to begin transferring the data. He hadn't been lying, exactly. Ikke really *was* the last one to show up on the Station's records—because he had edited them manually to ensure no trace of Enno's presence would remain. Zelkur wasn't planning on telling the patrolman. This was standard procedure for him. Any other long-term Station attendant would do the same.

That was not to say, of course, they were a part of a secret organized crime ring, or that they typically went out of their way to cover for pirates rushing through their systems. When you're alone on the far reaches of space where no one could hear you scream, Zelkur found it easier to get along with everybody, and avoid choosing a side as much as possible, even if that 'side' was the Space Patrol. After all, if something happened, Zelkur knew the *pirates* would be a hell of a lot more interested in following up with him than the Patrol. One of those was more likely to be fatal.

Enno's bunch had seemed like a decent lot, which was also why Zelkur was willing to quietly look the other way. Maybe they wouldn't hunt him down if he snitched, but a 'decent' pirate was hard to come by. There was no reason to get on their bad side.

The Dreker downloaded the report and tucked his pad away without looking at it, giving Zelkur a tip of the hat as he went. Zelkur waved him off with a newly-fueled tank (bought and paid for—even the most miserly bastard knew how much fuel cost out on the rim), and nothing in the way of leads. Zelkur privately thought this was a good thing regardless; Enno may have been willing to act friendly towards a Station Attendant while he was in need, but he doubted the Captain would be so accommodating to a couple of cops hounding his trail.

This, Zelkur concluded, was a case of 'All's well that ends well,' even if no one but him would know it.

When a refugee ship was the next thing to set off his alarms, Zelkur was grateful the one thing the Agus on board needed was fuel. There were enough beings on their ship to quickly eat *all* his supplies if they'd needed.

Fuel was something he could give, even if it cost him.

The problem was, they didn't have anything to pay him back.

"Do you take Agu currency?" Nunzad, the elected leader of the Agus, said hopefully, only to wilt when Zelkur shook his head.

"I don't need anything from you," he said firmly, if not unkindly. Zelkur could appreciate the intent, but keeping unmarked credits would only cause trouble for him in the long run. "Like I said, it's not often that I get visitors around here. Getting a chance to chat with y'all and hear what the wider universe is going through is good enough for me."

He *did* mean it, sincerely. His own needs were small, entertainment being the highest on the list. In the early days of his deployment, he'd thought he would never manage to get through all the books and shows he had downloaded onto his tablet. Recently, he'd found himself debating between binge-watching seven seasons of his favorite soap opera for the fourth time, or rereading the biology textbook from his college days that he'd accidentally thrown in with the rest of his things.

The Agu experience had injected some excitement into Zelkur's daily life, and he could ride that high for weeks.

His response didn't seem to be enough for the Agu. The three representatives quickly convened in a tight huddle, whispering together in a guttural tone.

At last, the leader returned with a determined expression that almost screamed he wouldn't be taking no for an answer.

"You said you spend most of your time here alone, yes? Just doing your duty?"

"That's right," Zelkur replied, raising a brow in question. It wasn't wrong—though there was an overestimation regarding just how much time was spent doing his 'duty' versus sitting around and waiting for his duty to be done.

"I'm sure that gets boring," the Agu said decisively, tilting their chin up stubbornly. "Not to show your position any disrespect, of course."

"No disrespect felt," Zelkur said, biting back a smile. "You're not wrong, after all."

"Good," they said and rummaged through the small knapsack. "I think I have something that may help."

They pulled out a thin tablet (proportional to their own size, but looking comically small to Zelkur's eyes) and clicked on the front, disengaging the lock before handing it off to Zelkur, along with a small bag including an equally small carrying case and charger.

"I'm sure it will be different from what you're used to," they said, nervously scratching the back of their head. "Books, music, movies, you name it. There're all sorts of genres with automatic translations into a number of languages, not just Agu and GalBas. There's thousands of different items to enjoy."

Zelkur cradled the tablet carefully in his hands, eyes wide. That was a *lot* more than he'd thought it would be—most personal pads weren't capable of storing more than a couple hundred things at once. This must be a special library tablet, something that continued to be rather rare for the common folk of the galaxy, regardless of the fact they made up the majority of the community.

"This is... this is *wonderful*, thank you," Zelkur said, uncharacteristically flustered. "I appreciate it. I'll try not to abuse the privilege."

Tablets like this could have their contents downloaded and repackaged easily, meaning a number of important cultural pieces could be sold and distributed without the owner's knowledge. While more knowledge in the galaxy was always a good thing, when it came to refugee groups like this, it could do a lot more harm than one might expect.

They trusted him.

All three of the Agus laughed, a small chuffing sound.

"You've saved all our lives!" Nunzad insisted. "If this is the only price we pay, we pay it gladly."

Zelkur huffed, smiling despite himself.

As always, he would do his best to live up to the expectation.

Android inspectors came by every couple of years, and Zelkur did his best to bear it gracefully. He knew it was a necessary part of the job, but the implied insult did rankle him a bit.

Most of the time, they would come onto his station without so much as a by-your-leave, secure in their position any Attendants would hesitate to shoot once they saw the company symbol on their jacket.

Not *this* inspector, though. They stayed firmly on their own ship, awaiting Zelkur's response.

There were plenty of people across the galaxy who had issues with androids—it hadn't been that long since the court case had successfully argued for their sentient rights.

Zelkur was of the opinion that someone who could do advanced math in their head, run entire space stations on their own, *and* shut down all arguments with vicious retorts (as one of his fellow Station Attendants did) was a fully sentient being, and anything about their status, physically speaking or otherwise, had absolutely nothing to do with him. As far as communication went, that Attendant was less inclined to direct contact than Zelkur was, but he read their commentary on the annual reports posted to the company bulletin. Their scathing words were always the highlight of the cycle.

To put it plainly, Zelkur understood why this particular android was expressing caution.

"You're welcome on this Station," Zelkur ducked his head, making sure the gesture was visible on the view screen. "I'll do what I can to accommodate you."

"Very well," the android said, their tone brisk. "Disembarking now."

The connection cut immediately, and Zelkur let out an amused huff. He was hardly one to stand on ceremony, and he appreciated a sense of straightforwardness in others. He'd hardly decided to strand himself on the far reaches of space because he put much stock in social niceties.

He rose from his seat and wandered towards the docking zone, making sure the inner-atmosphere would hold and no one would get sucked out into the cold void of space. Androids could survive many things but not that. Zelkur could survive far *less*, so he'd found it was best to take precautions.

The inspector walked unto the station, and Zelkur made sure to wipe his hand on a nearby towel before offering it to shake—he hardly wanted to start off on the wrong foot by smearing motor oil on his guest.

They shook his hand, firm with their three-fingered grip, and cleared their throat in a garbled, static sound.

"It's a pleasure. You may refer to me as TerigOn, representative of the Whitcomb Company. If my information is correct, you have been the on-site attendant for this location during the last fourteen pay periods, correct?"

"That is correct," Zelkur said agreeably, tossing the towel to rest over his shoulder. Had it really been fourteen years already? Wow. Time really *did* fly.

He stepped aside as TerigOn made their way into the station proper, whirling sensors moving about at a rapid pace.

"You have put forth two maintenance requests during that period," TerigOn noted, stopping by one of the display screens and accessing the database within. "Have there been no other problems during this period?"

"None that required me to access outside help," Zelkur said, which did *not* mean nothing ever happened.

"Understood," TerigOn said, and the way their optical sensors blinked purposefully indicated that they did, indeed, understand. An android would know the need for 'clandestine repairs' better than most.

There were a few more questions after that, all easily answered. Zelkur took his work seriously, after all. It was after TerigOn took a look at the ship's access records a spot of trouble popped up.

"You seem to have access to an online archive, but you have not logged this information in your latest report," the android noted.

Zelkur cleared his throat, feeling a bit sweaty despite himself. "Well, this isn't a resource I gained through company means, so it didn't seem relevant. It's just... stories. Books, shows, things like that. Nothing confidential, by any means."

"I see," TerigOn said. There was a quiet note of intrigue in their voice. "And these materials, you access them for free?"

Aha. Traveling the far reaches of space without much in the way of entertainment would get boring for anybody, no matter their species.

"Yup. Would you like me to download some for ya?" he offered, raising a brow in question. "The library's pretty extensive, and I've found a few I quite enjoyed so far."

TerigOn was still for a moment, servos whirring, before they nodded. "Yes, please. That would be acceptable."

Soon, Zelkur had TerigOn loaded back on their ship with a whole host of new reading materials and not a single question asked about where he'd gotten them.

A job well done, Zelkur would say.

If nothing else, the shared entertainment would smooth the way for further inspections. Zelkur had no idea what Enno could send in future drops. There had been a crate of live fish in one of them, and Zelkur had to wrangle for an hour before he could get them stored in the freezer. Being on the good side of an inspector would only benefit him.

Even if it didn't end up giving him extra benefits, Zelkur could content himself with the knowledge he had been able to pass on the Agus literature to a larger audience. Nunzad would be thrilled.

Knowledge was a benefit all on its own.

Of all the things for Ikke to arrive with when she came back to visit, a squirming, four-legged lizard with alarming dexterity and big, sad eyes was not what Zelkur expected.

"This is—"

"A Crax," Zelkur said, his interest piqued. "I remember seeing the diagrams from your latest research paper. Is it true they can survive up to thirty-five hours in antigravity?"

"More than that, I think," Ikke said, blinking as she adjusted her glasses. "I can only make observations based on natural occurrences, so it's difficult to gather data without the sort of extensive testing that would be needed to know for sure. You—You read my paper?"

"All of 'em," Zelkur corrected absently, scratching the Crax under the chin like Ikke's report noted as a pack member habit. "It's interesting stuff, Doc. Like the one on those weird raptors. Don't get much exposure to creatures with poison sacks out here. I liked that spitting attack you caught on camera, very spirited."

He had liked it so much, in fact, he had turned the spitting video into a 'gif' and enjoyed sending it as a 'reaction meme' when one of the other Station Attendants said something silly in their group chat. Zelkur pretended not to know what trendy terms meant, because it delighted him equally when the other Attendants got excited for a chance to explain something, or got overly huffy and embarrassed by his actions. Small blessings.

Ikke brightened, and she gave him a big, toothy grin. "I liked that one too! They're somewhat similar to a subsection of the lizard population in my home world, so I was quite eager to study them. I'm glad you find my work interesting! That'll make my purpose here a bit easier, I think."

Zelkur glanced back up at her, still providing the Crax with scratches. "This wasn't a social visit, then?"

"Partly," Ikke laughed. "It's not an obligation, by any means. But I do have a favor to ask you."

Zelkur leaned back, taking his hand away and valiantly ignoring the Crax's whines, though the scaly head bumping piteously against his leg made it hard. "A favor? I don't know how much I can do for ya, but I'm happy to do what I can."

"It's not much," she waved her hands through the air dismissively, looking a touch flustered. "At least, it *shouldn't* be. But it would be a huge help in my research, and if everything goes well, I could put you down as a contributor for my next paper!"

Ah. Something to do with her paper? And with her current line of study—

Zelkur glanced back down at the Crax drooling steadily against his knee and looking at him with big, wet eyes.

"I'm guessing ya need me to look after Fido here, for a bit?"

Ikke clasped her hands together as she nodded, looking a little sheepish. "Yes, that's exactly it. I've been looking into their camouflage abilities and how they can adapt in different environments. A ship like this is contained, and you already have everything that a Crax would need to thrive!"

"Don't they need exercise?" Zelkur said, a touch skeptical.

Ikke shook her head. "They're a largely sedate species. This one is just excited right now."

Zelkur sighed, already able to tell where this was going. "What would you need me to *do*, exactly?"

"Tell me what they're doing when I call! Anecdotal evidence is valuable, especially when I can't be everywhere at once. Observed behavior matters, even if it's not observed by a licensed professional. I promise, it won't add anything significant to your work hours..." she trailed off, smiling sheepishly. "Would you mind?"

Zelkur looked down at the Crax. It laid its head against his knee, and two long tongues drooped out of its mouth, promptly licking its own eyeball.

Zelkur melted.

"It can't be more trouble than any *other* guest I've gotten recently," he grumbled.

"Don't worry!" Ikke laughed and winked at him. "Given the nature of what I'm studying, you probably won't *notice* it half the time."

"Sounds like it," Zelkur sighed, only partially put-upon.

The station *had* been getting a bit boring lately. Zelkur's species could live for another hundred years if he ate healthy and exercised more. With a new companion on-board, he would have an excuse to do both.

Well, Zelkur reflected as the Crax rolled around in a pile of nearby laundry and Ikke tried to contain her giggles, if he was going to be stuck on the ass-end of space for another century, this wouldn't be the worst way to spend his time.

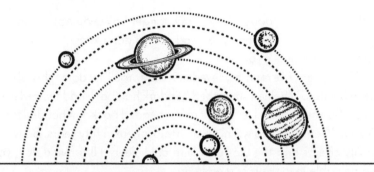

Real Time: A Story of the Thousand Year War

By S.L. Field

Seventeen had not been a good year for Jen Kuchner the first time around. She wasn't thrilled to wake up in Iverson Deep Space Transit Station and find cold sleep had bio-reset her body as a teenager, complete with teenage hormones. This time, she was in the middle of nowhere.

As a contract linguist embedded with Earth's Combined Military Forces, Jen joined Zheleen Cruz on the night shift in Iverson's operations center. They worked from 1900 in "the evening" to 0700 in "the morning." Every. Single. Day.

Jen lived in a grey metallic tube and wore grey coveralls with the company name "SpaceTech Protection Services" on the back. Religious services were temporal landmarks in the monotony of Iverson, so they were heavily attended by the faithful and bored alike. Other landmarks included ice cream on Fridays and laundry on Wednesdays. On Tuesdays, the day shift worked an extra two hours to give the night shift more free time, and on Thursdays "J & Z" reciprocated. Unless something interesting happened on shift, that was it.

"I sure hope the money they're paying us makes this gig worth it," Jen said one evening before work as she and Zheleen lounged in the military park. Feet propped on a planter, she gazed at the imitation blue sky dotted with picturesque clouds. "How much longer have you got again, Z? I'm going to be screwed when you head back. I don't know how you pick up on transmissions like you do."

"Four years, five months, seventeen days. You'll be doing this job in your sleep by then." Zheleen smoothed her dark hair back and twisted it into a messy bun held by a silver clip. "I'm not headed back, I'm headed forward. Proxima Centauri Two will have an atmosphere in fifty years. Between relativity effects and the bio-reset with cold sleep, I'll arrive a rich, young woman able to look up at a real sky."

"Not afraid the enemy will get you?" Jen raised an eyebrow, thinking of the loathsome, trollish, vaguely hominid species that had been plaguing humanity for decades. "You know they eat people."

"Nope. It's my job to know where the Tronnies are and call Special Operations down on them. Yours too, so let's get to it." Zheleen popped up and strode off to the operations center. "Are you staying awake for church or going to replay it in the afternoon? If you're staying up, we could watch together after breakfast," she called back, moving with uncharacteristic speed.

"I'll pass. I'd make myself stay awake until 0930 if command allowed us to attend in person, but if we have to stream it, I'll do it on my own time," Jen groused. The damned military personnel could go to the civilian section of the station whenever they wanted but not the contract linguists.

"Yeah well, security has a point. The civilian decks can turn rough depending on which ships are docked. Still, I've gotta stream church live or I can't hear it. Just like monitoring Tronate communications—the closer to real time, the better." Zheleen let the security checkpoint beams scan her before entering the corridor to the military operations center.

"That's crazy, Z. Transmissions don't get clearer depending on how close to real time you run them, and streaming church live won't make Pastor Julie's accent less thick. I'd think after six years you'd be used to it." Jen had to jog to catch up with Zheleen as they entered the operations center. It was a vast, dim space lit by the screens on the desks and fairy lights strung across the ceiling. Jen had no idea why they were up there, but she liked them. She liked the black and cobalt blue fatigues of the soldiers too—a sure sign her dull grey coveralls were wearing on her.

Toby, the senior linguist on the day shift, bounced up from his chair as they approached. "Wow, you guys must have read my mind. I was hoping

you'd get in early. Can you figure out what's up with this signal? It origi-
nates 100 kilometers from Jump Site Delta, but supposedly there's nothing
out there. Delta won't open for traffic until Thursday. The signal is like
static, but ten minutes ago, I swore I heard whispering beneath the crackle.
Creeps me out."

"Everything creeps you out, Toby," Delia. the other day shift linguist
said and stretched her manicured fingers towards the fairy lights. She wore
a silky grey tunic outfit with a pin on her breast displaying the SpaceTech
Protection seal. Delia loved to test the limits of the company's vague
dictum, *Contractors shall wear grey, functional clothing appropriate to their
postings with the SpaceTech logo clearly displayed thereon*. Sometimes the
bosses called her on it, sometimes not.

"Space is a creepy place, Deels," Toby snapped. He stepped aside to
let Z sit in his chair. "Just listen, Z."

Everyone stared at Zheleen. She was the longest serving linguist at the
station and had ears like a bat.

Toby touched the screen. A waveform appeared. "Here's where I
thought I heard whispering. Am I crazy?"

Zheleen put her headsets on and closed her eyes. No one breathed.

"I hear something," she muttered, playing with the dials to repeat and
filter the playback. "Possibly Tronate Dialect C from the pitch, but I can't
catch the words." She jabbed the arrow on the screen to take her to the
live signal and gave a relieved sigh, but kept listening, nodding her head
as if in time to words passing through her ears.

"Dialect C with some unfamiliar words, maybe a different cohort than
we've encountered so far." Zheleen frowned, kept listening. After a bit she
added, "Small craft . . . two on board . . . positioned to spot ships emerging
from Delta as soon as they appear."

Zheleen flipped the headset onto the desk. "Spotter skiff but working
harder to shield their comms than usual. What's out of Delta next, Chief?"

Chief Boggs, the military-side space traffic controller, wandered over
from his workstation and checked the screen. "A water shipment from
Triton is coming in for crew break and resupply as soon as Delta opens for
incoming traffic. Man, we've got to put more security on these big water
haulers. This is the Tronnies' third attempt this year."

"Yup, well, we're on it. Jen and I will process the traffic and do a report.
Special Operations can take action from there." Zheleen looked up and

smiled. "Nice outfit, Delia. Shoot me the specs and I'll find out if one of the vendors on the promenade will make me something not, you know, awful."

Jen took over Delia's station and started to scan the expected signals transiting the region to ensure nothing weird was piggybacking off them.

"How do you do that, Z?" she asked, pulling up a transmission wave-form and running diagnostics against it.

"You've got to get close, is all," Zheleen said, putting her headset back on.

————————

There were no breaks during the late shift. Jen covered the routine traffic channels, and Zheleen wrote a report and monitored the enemy skiff. Meanwhile, a cruiser maneuvered a squad of SpecOps towards it. Zheleen suggested they kill the target, but the commander wanted to seize the Tronnies for interrogation. The cruiser had just obtained a visual on the enemy skiff when Toby and Delia returned.

Delia, wearing a sleek dark grey bodysuit with the SpaceTech logo and flowers in lighter greys scattered across it, stared at the skiff on the main screen. "Damn, how did they squeeze two of those big trolls on that ship?" she wondered.

Toby shook his head. "Better question is how the Tronnies maneuvered it. They're dumb as rocks; every one I've monitored."

"Maybe, but whatever's giving them orders isn't. We have no idea what those 'masters' they're so terrified of are like," Zheleen shook her head. "Each interrogation report has wildly different descriptions—like the Tronnies made them up on the spot. Or like the masters can appear as anything."

"Shit, what a creepy thought, Z." Toby shuddered. "The trolls are bad enough. I sure as hell don't want to interrogate one."

"Signal's gone dead," Delia announced.

"Well, I'm out," Zheleen said. "We won't know how this operation ends for hours. I can't hang that long. Toby, if the signal comes back, stay on it in real time. If you agree that boarding is a bad idea, check if Ivanov or Wang can convince the commander. I sure struck out."

Jen left with Zheleen, surprised at how drawn she looked. Ten minutes later they arrived in crew quarters: metal boxes big enough for a narrow bed, a locker, and a sink. One shared shower for every four rooms made a "quad." They reached Zheleen's door first.

"For once, I'm going to follow your lead and do church after I get some sleep. I've been focusing so hard, I think my brain is going to melt out of my ears. See you for dinner," Zheleen said as the door closed.

"Yeah, go rest. You look wrecked," Jen replied.

In her own room, Jen washed, put on pink pajamas with white kittens cavorting on them. They were much like a set her daughter Annie had worn when she was seventeen. Looking in the mirror, Jen blinked at her resemblance to Annie, but something else struck her, too. Her blue eyes were still sharp. She looked like a youngster with juice left in her, even after the difficult shift. Unlike Zheleen, she never pushed herself.

She remembered Zheleen struggling with the audio Toby had given her, then jumping to the live feed before she could make anything out.

"You've got to get close," Zheleen had said. *She meant close in real time*, Jen thought. Z always pushed her to listen to live transmissions, but for some reason, Jen was reluctant. Scared, even. She told the young face in the mirror, "I'll stay up for church and find out if Z is right about understanding Pastor Julie better live. I mean, it's church, right? No soldiers are going out on mission based on what I hear."

Jen realized she was starving. She pulled her coveralls back on over her pajamas and dashed to the mess hall. Breakfast was in full swing and soldiers from the ops center motioned her over. She almost caved. That adorable Sergeant Yoshihiro Ivanov was there—damn teenage hormones! —but her determination to stream church live prevailed. Jen grabbed a breakfast sandwich and sprinted back, arriving just in time to jump into bed, prop the computer screen on her lap, and start the feed from the interfaith center. It felt irreverent to her, but that was life in deep space.

After the opening hymn Pastor Julie (day job, resupply supervisor) stepped forward dressed in blue robes with a white sash. She started her generic "all Christians" service with John 3:16, arms held high, declaring in her thick Mars Homesteader accent, "For God so loved the world..."

Jen understood every word and felt uplifted despite how rote the verse had become.

Next, Julie welcomed those in the room and throughout the station as the camera pulled back to show the congregation.

Jen loved the long shots. The interfaith center's huge screens lit up like stained glass windows along the walls, and showed the other contractors who lived in relative freedom—and nicer clothes—on the civilian decks of Iverson. Since Jen rarely understood most of what Pastor Julie said, her attention stayed on people watching. Not this time, though. Julie's words remained.

"This week we welcome the NAAS *Milton*, headed to Proxima Centauri Two. I am also happy to see CCAS *Shandong* crew back this week." She smiled as the congregation clapped for each ship. "Let us pray for the Maersk *Chattanooga* safe passage, scheduled to arrive on Thursday." She clasped her hands to her breast. "Almighty saving Lord, preserve the *Chattanooga* and its crew…"

A snort and a nasty laugh from somewhere in the congregation, followed by a derisive, "Po' Pasta' Jul gonna be cry come Tursday" in outer-planet jargon made Jen bolt upright in her bed. The microphones were directed at Pastor Julie on the dais, with congregation noises muted. Yet this voice had been as clear as if she were in the room.

And then she was.

Frozen, gasping in shallow breaths, Jen stood in the second row surrounded by translucent congregants, like poorly projected holograms of themselves. Except one. The tall man with the painful skinniness of an asteroid miner stood beside her, as real as she was.

"Oh my," he turned and looked down at her. "You a pretty yo'ng listena. See what real, don you? Looka dis!"

The man swept an arm towards the wall and the stained-glass screens transformed to show a cratered asteroid surrounded by stars. Four figures in SpecOps space suits staggered towards the edge of the asteroid, their face shields shattered. They kept going past the sharp edge and out into space. Drifting at first, they soon shot off like comets to disappear among the stars.

Jen stared, unable to breath. The man turned back and ran his hand down her cheek. It seared her like flame.

"You needa be mo' careful, hoonee, or soon you be like you dark-hair frien an' dose spaca-soldas dere. You get *too* close, you die."

The scream that tore from Jen's throat launched her back into her bed. Still screaming, she slapped the computer screen away with such force she slid off the bed to the floor. Scrambling up, she shot into the corridor in her pajamas and bare feet and flung herself against Zheleen's door.

"Zheleen! Zheleeeennnn! Z... Zee...Zeeee..." She pounded the door, then stepped back, and kicked it with her bare foot. Pain lancing up her leg and terror of Zheleen not answering—and nor anyone else, since most of the section worked days—made her scream again.

Collapsed against the bulkhead, Jen stared at her own door. Her computer and datalink were inside, but the thought of going back made her heart race and her hands tremble. "Please don't be dead, Zheleen," Jen whispered. "I'll call for help. I'll try." She began to limp back towards her door, braced with resolve.

"Jen Kuchner? What happened?"

Jen twisted around to behold Yoshihiro Ivanov running towards her from two quads away in his fatigue pants and black undershirt. Behind him stood Jen and Zheleen's nearest night-shift neighbor, Melly, wearing an exasperated expression and not much else.

"She just had some big fight with her bestie, Yoshi. She'll be *fine*," Melly groused.

Ivanov glanced back. "I'll take care of this, Melly. Get back in the room."

Melly left with a huffy sigh, her door swishing shut.

Ivanov turned to Jen and approached gingerly, as people approach a crazy person they don't want to set off. "Jen, *did* you have a fight with Zheleen? Did you hit each other? Because you don't look so good, kid."

Jen hesitated, afraid she'd wind up in the psych ward on level six if she told the truth. She needed time to think. "I'm not a kid. I'm, like, forty. Ish." Jen glanced down at her kitty jammies, knowing they didn't help her case— and saw her grotesquely swollen foot.

"Oh my God!" she blurted.

"How did that happen, Jen? And your cheek?"

Ivanov was close now, alert and wary. Jen realized he was no more "adorable" than she was seventeen years old. No one landed at Iverson without water under their bridge.

"What about my cheek?" she raised her hands to her face, but immediately snatched it away. Her cheek was on fire. "Oh no," she gasped, "That man was *real*. We have to get Zheleen out of there!"

"Who was real, Jen? Why do you think Zheleen is in danger?"

Ivanov slid a datalink into his pocket. Jen knew he had signaled for help.

"Tell me what you think happened, Jen. Don't worry about sounding crazy, crazy shit is all over this place. Tell me, so I can get authorization to force her door." Ivanov's voice sounded both reassuring and commanding.

Jen wavered for a second, then everything burst out—Zheleen heading into her room in total exhaustion, the church service, the nightmare—or vision—of SpecOps soldiers staggering to their deaths, and the implication that Zheleen was dead. How the terrifying man had stroked her cheek. As Jen finished sobbing and babbling, two EMTs showed up. *This is it*, she thought, *straight to the psych ward. But Zheleen. . .*

Jen grabbed Ivanov's wrists. "Zheleen hasn't answered her door, even though the noise brought you here from two quads away when you had, uh, better things to do. Please, please check on her and I'll go quietly."

Ivanov looked hard at Jen and retrieved his datalink.

"Keep an eye on her and check her injuries. Especially that cheek," he ordered the EMTs. Then, into the datalink, "Sergeant Yoshihiro Ivanov, operations center security detail, requesting emergency entry to a residential pod based on a credible suspicion of illness or injury. Resident is non-responsive." He held his link up to the datamatrix box beside Zheleen's door, and it slid open.

Zheleen lay face down on the floor. She hadn't made it two steps inside.

————————

The lights were too bright. Jen could see them through her eyelids and put her hands over her eyes, shouting "Dim lights!"

What's on my cheek? A bandage? Sitting bolt upright, Jen squinted. She was in a medical ward with two beds. *The psych ward*, she thought with a pang of terror. Zheleen occupied the other bed, and as Jen watched, she rolled on her side and pulled the sheet over her head.

"What happened to us?" Jen whispered.

The door swished open, and the adorable Sergeant Yoshihiro Ivanov walked in—except he looked older and tougher now. *When did that transformation happen?*

"Welcome back, Jen. I thought if we got the lights bright enough, you'd come to."

"Turn them down, they're awful . . . Wait, what are you doing here? And why aren't you adorable anymore?" Jen's hands flew to her mouth in horror. *Did I say that out loud?*

Ivanov burst out laughing but ordered the lights down. The room technology paid more attention to him.

"Bio-Age resets give me time at each new post to come across as a young, decorative lightweight. I prefer to be underestimated, so I'm glad that was your first impression." Ivanov took a seat beside her bed. "You're seeing things you didn't see before, and it happened fast, not even a year into your contract. Do you remember why you're here, Jen?"

Jen shook her head.

"You broke your foot. Do you remember?"

Jen swung her legs from under the sheet, and sure enough, her right foot was in a flexicast. She broke out in cold sweat. She was afraid to know what had happened. *Why?*

"I . . . I . . . can't remember," she mumbled.

"It's difficult after a big trauma and sedation, but try to recall on your own. What happened to your cheek?"

Jen lifted her hand to her left cheek. It hurt under the thick dressing.

"The asteroid miner touched it, and it felt like fire. He told me that I had to be careful or I would die like Zheleen and the SpecOp soldiers who drifted off into space." Jen bit her lip, everything rushing back like a wave crashing into her mind. "But Zheleen isn't dead, so was I dreaming, or—am I crazy?"

"Zheleen *was* dead. The EMTs got her heart and breathing restarted, and thanks to the docs, there won't be any brain damage. She's going to sleep about fourteen hours a day for the next week, and Toby and Delia need help. We need to try and clear you for duty. Can you do that?"

Jen stared straight ahead, cold as ice, trying to assimilate everything, then blurted, "She died at the same time as those soldiers. They were the SpecOps sent to board the enemy skiff. What happened?"

"The skiff blew up as they approached, while the church service was going on—if I had to bet, at the exact time you encountered that man." Ivanov gave a one-shouldered shrug. "It's what happens whenever a Tronate linguist crosses over: you see what's real, even if you don't see it in this, I dunno, ordinary world."

"How do you know these things? What is 'crossing over'?" Jen feared her trembling might shake her off the bed.

Ivanov grabbed her frozen hands and covered them with his. "I'm sorry this is so hard for you. What happened tends to take much longer and comes on gradually so the senior linguists can talk you through it. I know this stuff because my main job on station security is to keep an eye on linguists, and I've been doing it—here and on Ganymede and ProxTwo—for thirty years of actual, on-post time. Tronate linguists are one of our most valuable survival assets, as rare as hens' teeth, and you burn out at a fantastic rate. 'Crossing over' is when we receive intel reports from a linguist that can't be deduced from the word-for-word translations. Thing is, we've learned you people aren't making shit up. Ninety percent of the time, the reports turn out to be true." Ivanov sighed. "I'm going to arrange some food. The toilet is over there, let me help you up. Careful with your foot."

He held Jen under her elbow until she could manage.

"Hey, what day is it?" She asked as Ivanov turned to leave.

"Wednesday, about 0900."

"What? *Wednesday?*" Jen's voice rose and her breathing sped up.

"Yeah... Wait, what's the matter? Why are you afraid?" Ivanov's eyes narrowed.

"We have to do something. The Maersk *Chattanooga* arrives first thing tomorrow. The enemy is going to destroy it."

Eventually Ivanov returned to the ward, pushing a roller cart with baked oatmeal, grooming supplies, clean underwear, and her horrible SpaceTech coverall.

"I warned the crew at the ops center about the *Chattanooga*. Makes sense, that's the first ship coming through Delta Jump Site, and it's the one the skiff was waiting for. You think the threat is still active? The commander isn't convinced."

"Yes," Jen swallowed a bite of oatmeal. "This is great."

"Eat and talk, Jen. The enemy skiff is gone, and Toby and Delia swear the crew had no idea it was going to explode. Looks like an accident, but still, the enemy knows we're on to them and we're pissed about our dead soldiers. They normally back off. Why not this time?"

"Because the man at church laughed at Pastor Julie when she gave a blessing for the *Chattanooga*. He said she was going to cry on Thursday. He knew about the SpecOps and didn't care. He seemed pretty happy about it, in fact. Bastard. What did he do to my cheek?" She poked at the bandage again. *Ouch! I've got to stop doing that.*

"Electrical burn. The damage is deep. You'll have that dressing on for a while." Ivanov pulled a data pad from the cart, tapped at it, and showed it to her. "This is the service when Pastor Julie gave her blessing. Is your man in here?"

Jen braced herself before looking, but as soon as her eyes hit the screen, she knew.

"He's not there."

"You're sure? Nowhere in the room?"

"I think I was in a place that only looked like the interfaith center. Like a holodeck or simulation room. I just didn't realize it. The man looked like an asteroid miner I saw in a horror movie that terrified me as a kid. That's how I interpreted the presence of the enemy." Things were becoming clearer to Jen by the second.

Ivanov nodded. "Amazing insight, Jen. It took years for the first crossed-over linguists to figure out their minds were representing alien phenomena and messages in familiar terms."

"Wait," Jen said. "Run the vid, I think I missed something."

"I think so too." Zheleen wobbled over in her hospital gown.

Jen scooched over to let her sit and wrapped an arm around her. "Are you okay?" her voice cracked.

"Okay enough. Keep your arm around me. Physical contact between crossed-over linguists helps. Run it, Yoshi." Z was all business.

Jen dropped her arm. "You knew this stuff about linguists getting psychic and that security—Ivanov! —was in on it?"

"Yes, but no one can tell you about it. You have to discover it for yourself. All I could do was push you to focus and get closer to real time while monitoring transmissions. I never dreamed it would hit you so soon, or that a church service would push you over. As for Yoshi," Zheleen gave a faint smile, "Your crush on him was so cute, why take that away from you?" She put her arm around Jen and repeated, "Run it."

Pastor Julie clasped her hands for the blessing again. No nasty comments or laughing interrupted. Jen scanned the congregants in the row where she had stood.

"Hey, these guys are all NAAS *Milton* crew, the whole second row," Jen said, tapping the screen.

As Pastor Julie finished, one of the *Milton* crewmen put his hand up and said something inaudible. It became clear, though, when Julie replied, "Of course. Let us also ask a blessing on the *Milton*, which got a change of orders to depart Wednesday. Oh, mighty and loving God..."

"That's it!" Zheleen cried. "The enemy distracted you to make sure you didn't hear that part. Everything with the spotter skiff and the explosion had to be a misdirection to make us think we'd countered the threat. The enemy has coopted the *Milton* with plans to kill the *Chattanooga*. As North American Alliance Space Corp, they're armed to the teeth. No merchant ship stands a chance against them. But why kill it? Doesn't the enemy want the water?"

She sagged against Jen suddenly.

"Z, you're done. Back into bed now and stay in this world." Ivanov got Zheleen to her bed, calling in a nurse to sedate her. "No meditating, considering possibilities, or dreaming."

"We can't be too careful when you guys get overextended," he explained to Jen. "You're on. Get dressed."

As Jen fumbled to force her cast through her coverall leg, Ivanov called Chief Boggs at traffic control. "What is the NAAS *Milton* doing now?... No! Stop it, keep the docking clamps on...Then *tell* the fucking commander, but secure that ship first, and send Marines out there."

Ivanov dropped to a knee and got Jen's station boot on her left foot. The right foot was a lost cause. "You'll have to maneuver as best you can in zero grav with one magnetic boot," he said.

"Wait, did the ops center somehow lose gravity?" Jen exclaimed, forgetting the whole station would have had to stop rotating for that to happen.

"We're not going there. I want you as close as possible to pinpoint where the enemy influence is on the *Milton*. We're headed to the space dock."

Jen floated in the zero grav of Iverson's vast docking bay. She was attached to the deck by her magnetized left boot. Several station Marines were arrayed behind her, ready to board the *Milton*, while the *Milton's* Marines stood just beyond the ship's open airlock, ready to stop them. Ivanov and the *Milton's* exec stood between them, screaming at each other. The plan was for Jen to search the ship for "contraband" and see what impressions she could get, but the plan was stalled.

Jen caught the eye of a particularly young-looking ship's marine. He fixated on her, and it struck Jen that she could influence him. She detached her boot from the deck and floated over the startled Marines.

"Come on, I'll show you where that contraband is so your ship can get underway," she said and grabbed his arm. He followed her. And no one chased them. A little voice in the back of her mind whispered she would have to investigate the parameters of this newfound persuasive ability.

Jen and the Marine, a red-headed corporal in North American Alliance blue fatigues, floated past battened-down quarters and storage areas. An aura of fear and unreality grew every meter they progressed, and Jen tracked it like a bloodhound. As they approached the bridge, Jen discovered she could not just sense it, but *smell* it, like mold and decay, and see it like a faint grey-green mist trailing along the corridors.

"Do you see that mist, Corporal O'Brian?" Jen asked at one point, checking the name on his uniform.

He shook his head, eyes slightly anxious, but still fixed and wide as if hypnotized. Jen glanced back along their path. "Where is everyone?"

"Secured for departure, ma'am. We'll go as soon as you find the contraband," he responded in the deferential tone soldiers used to address senior officers.

Weird, Jen thought as she grabbed a handhold on the bulkhead to stop herself. The greenish trail disappeared into a closed door beside them. The secured entrance to the bridge was straight ahead, the stench overwhelming. "We're here."

Jen and her Marine reattached their boots to the metallic deck with matching clicks. "You should pull your weapon out, Corporal, and take the safety off."

O'Brien did so before she finished speaking, but his face radiated distress, and he was breathing hard. Jen saw Ivanov and the ship's exec float around the corner—so they had tracked her, after all—and shook her head at them. She put her hand on the corporal's shoulder. "What's in there? Can you open this door?"

"Yes, ma'am. It's the breakroom for the bridge officers. I... I don't want to go in there."

It occurred to Jen while the corporal might not be able to smell the stench or see the trail, he sensed something, and he was afraid. Much more afraid than she might have expected from a Marine on his own ship escorting a young, unarmed woman looking for contraband— then it hit her, too. Not her own organic fear, but something pushing on her and O'Brian from the breakroom. Jen visualized herself pushing it back, as if forcing a door shut. After a minute, the extreme terror receded, but her own entirely reasonable fear remained. *I have to brace myself—and him.*

Jen squeezed O'Brian's shoulder. "This is weird, and I'm scared too, but we have to kill the enemy. It's in there."

"I thought we were looking for contraband." O'Brien's voice shook. "There's no room for a Tronnie in there, they're huge!"

"No, only the trolls are, the sort of humanoid ones. I think the masters can be small. I think maybe they can be anything. All they need is an anchor in our world." Jen tried to make her voice confident. It wasn't easy. "So, we go through this door, and I track down where that thing's hiding. When I say 'Shoot,' do it no matter what you see."

The door swished open suddenly, and Jen and the corporal gasped. The ship's exec had put his palm on the door plate. Ivanov stood behind him, sidearm out, and both men nodded. Jen detached her boot and launched into the small cabin, following the mist trail to a cabinet over the coffee station. She took three quick breaths, flung the door open before she lost her nerve, and shouted, "Shoot!"

The motion threw her backwards in the zero grav to bump against the bulkhead as shots rang out one after another.

O'Brien must have emptied his magazine into whatever was in the cabinet, but as Jen tried to stabilize herself, the breakroom faded. She now stood on the dream-world asteroid while the gaunt "miner" screeched and kicked her. Each time a kick connected with her legs, pain exploded over Jen's entire body, and she staggered backwards. The creature pursued her, landing more kicks. Jen realized she could die in this nightmare place. Would that be the end of her in the "real" world, too? She didn't want to find out.

Jen stopped and waited, and the miner charged. At the last second, she stepped aside, grabbed the creature by its skinny arm and swung it off the asteroid. Twenty meters into space it exploded, throwing her back into the breakroom on the *Milton*. A mottled, toad-like creature with too many legs and eyes floated in round globules of umber blood and chunks of flesh blasted off by the corporal's sustained fire. As she stared at the gruesome sight, her world dimmed to black.

Jen woke up in the Med ward—this was getting old. Zheleen sat in the chair next to her in a cute pale grey dress with a SpaceTech Protection pin.

"I've worked here six years trying to understand why we're getting our asses kicked by big, stupid trolls. Then you show up and in a few months crossed over during a church service. Three days after that, you discovered we're really fighting toads the size of Labrador dogs with three eyes on each side of their heads and psychic powers. Geez, Jen! I had to make Yoshi take me shopping in the civilian section to get over how you showed me up."

Jen struggled to sit, babbling an insight so compelling, it was as if she had awakened only to share it.

"Z, it has to happen all at once. I killed the creature in that dream place because the Marine shot the toad thing here. Is he okay? Corporal O'Brien, not the toad."

"Sort of. He's been in the brig for letting you on the ship, but the *Milton's* still stuck at Iverson while security goes over every centimeter of the ship and grills the crew about their 'change of orders.' Seems they thought the first ship through Delta would be an enemy transport. You'll be next under the microscope, but they need us linguists, Jen—every precious one of us— so set some terms. Make them take you shopping, at least! Maybe visit your Marine in the brig, too, once you get med clearance."

"He was kind of adorable." Jen smiled, but it quickly faded. "I've been out for a *week*, Z? What happened, did I...die? Like you did? Does that happen a lot? I'm not sure I want to play this game, if that's the deal."

"That's not the deal—at least we don't think so. You were just exhausted after tracking that creature, like we all get when we overdo it. Since you already had issues with your foot and cheek, plus a bunch of hideous new bruises on your legs, the doctors kept you in delta wave sleep so you could recover faster. Also, Yoshi wanted to keep the military inquisition off you as long as possible."

"Okay," Jen replied uncertainly, fingering the light "second skin" dressing which had replaced the bulky layers on her cheek. "We've been recovering all this time and Toby and Delia have been alone? I bet they're pissed! When can we go back on duty? Do we know why the enemy went so far as to infiltrate one of our ships? And why they wanted to destroy the *Chattanooga* instead of taking it?"

"The *Chattanooga* had a secret cargo—more linguists," Zheleen answered the last question first. "Turns out, the enemy fears us, which makes us more valuable than ever, and more desperately needed. You'll have twelve more hours to rest, then you start helping train the newbie linguists, telling them what you saw and answering a zillion questions for the intel types and psychologists."

"Shit, Z, it's like that? They'll never let our contracts expire now. We've got a long haul ahead of us."

"Yeah, it's like that. I'm not sure we even *have* contracts anymore. I bet you anything the Combined Forces will draft us to serve 'indefinitely, according to the needs of the service.'" Zheleen looked down at the floor and bit her lip. "Jen, you found that thing. You tracked it and saw it in that dream place and here. What do you think? What are we facing? I mean, now that we know who the toad masters are, can we beat them?" Zheleen finished in a whisper. A worried, doubtful whisper.

Jen's head spun. She closed her eyes to keep the room from fading and gripped the sides of her mattress while unbidden images flashed through her head so fast, she could only grasp a few disconnected fragments. "Stop!" she shouted at last, and the visions did—with a physical jolt.

Jen opened her eyes. Zheleen had grabbed her hand so tightly it was turning white.

"It's forever, isn't it?" Zheleen said. "No creature in this world is the real enemy, they're just tools. The real enemy is...different. It doesn't live in time." Her tone indicated she had guessed at this but hadn't wanted to face it.

"Yeah," Jen nodded. "But won't be *forever* for us. Even if we keep moving linguists from star system to star system, they'll keep us young and working until we hit our last walls. We'll have to learn to take care of each other, and make sure we get something in return—and I don't mean just cute clothes and promenade visits. The command has to let us develop real training and recruit more people. A lot more, because..." Jen shivered as all traces of her brief flirtation with teenage silliness slipped away, "as far as I can see, the war will last a thousand years."

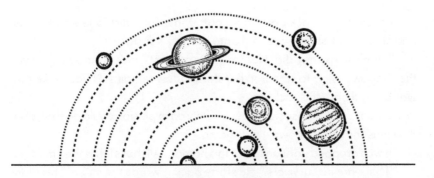

The Last Story

By Mohammad Khan

O n a cloudy day, the tall grasses sway aggressively from a descending hovercraft as it lands in a large crater.

The large door opens. Two humans walk out of the craft wearing steel gray suits and helmets. One holds up a device, scanning the area. It nods, and they remove their helmets. Green grasslands surround the white dirt-filled crater. Their craft pales in comparison to the size of the crater.

"What do you think this is?" says Largoto. He holds his helmet under his arm as he squints, looking for signs of life. "Where are the inhabitants? I don't see any reason to remain in this silly form and speak their language if the inhabitants are not here."

"I think I'll remain in this form," says Loyola. "Respect the dead. We might run into a local. Wouldn't want to scare them off."

She walks around, occasionally sifting through the sand with her fingers.

Largoto takes out his scanner. It starts clicking rapidly. "Whoa, whoa," says Largoto. "I'm getting radioactivity all over the place."

"How bad?"

"Nothing we can't handle," he says with worry and inquisition. "But how did *they*? I mean, what lived here that could handle it."

Loyola sees a rock protruding out of the white dirt. She walks closer and sees a dark shadow seared onto the rock's surface.

"I don't think they did. Not for long, at least." Her hand sweeps over the shadow, trying to smear it, but the shadow remains. "It looks like this was burned onto this rock.'

Largoto walks closer to inspect. "Only an explosion could do that, and they must not have known it was going."

"It was dropped right on top of this human. All that's left is this smudge."

"There are no survivors." He starts back towards the ship. "This planet's a wasteland."

"No," says Loyola. "Our mission was to report what we find."

"And we found nothing. They're dead. Every being is dead."

"You don't know that. There could be more in hiding."

"Fine", grumbles Largoto. "Let's search for the rest."

———————

Their craft traverses over the land with ease. It passes elk, caribou, vultures, monkeys, and tigers until it stops at an abandoned factory slightly covered in snow. They land in a forest near a bridge.

Largoto walks to a sign marked "Bridge of Death: Chernobyl Nuclear Disaster."

"We were right," he starts. "It was a nuclear disaster at someplace called Chernobyl."

Loyola scans the sign with a gadget. "The sign is over 300 years old."

Largoto walks to the bridge. "This was a bridge of death for a reason," he says to himself. He jumps on the bridge. "There's nothing wrong with it. Seems structurally fine."

Loyola searches for clues from the bridge and sees a building in the distance. "There." She points. "It could be that building. They could have died from radiation poisoning or burns from that building."

"They watched a nuclear explosion from the bridge. Surely, they deserved to die off. There are no beings there. Let's go."

"We need to document why they are gone. It could be the cause."

"A big bright flash in the sky wasn't warning enough? Did that need a sign?"

Loyola ignores him as they walk back to the craft. She spots something in the grass of the forest. A muddied doll lies with braided yellow hair and buttoned eyes. She scans the doll; her detector clicks rapidly.

"What is that?"

Loyola holds the doll. "I dunno. Maybe a young one's toy."

She keeps the doll with her. They walk back to their craft as Largoto mumbles about the stupidity of the human race.

Their hovercraft wavers as it lands near the Chernobyl power plant. They walk out with their radiation counters clicking erratically.

A large building shrouded in metal stands before them along an abandoned cooling tower.

Largoto holds his scanner towards the power plant. "Wow, the structure is extremely radioactive."

Loyola walks closer to the building with her scanner. She looks at her device. "How old is the radiation? How much decay has happened?"

Largoto pushes buttons on his device. "Uranium approximately 3000 years decayed."

"The radiation off this building is 5000 years *along* with 3000 years."

"There were TWO nuclear explosions?"

"They seemed to have contained the first one." She sees a hole into the building and shines a flashlight into the abyss. "Let's see where it began."

"Why? We know the nuclear explosion killed them off. If not, the radiation poisoning. Our job's done."

"But we don't know why." Loyola stands at the edge of the abyss, facing Largoto. "We need to know why."

She dons her helmet and heads into the darkness. Largoto follows her.

In the basement of Chernobyl, the walls slowly drip with contaminated water. The hallways and rooms have caved in. Largoto's radiation detector goes haywire as they peer around the corner.

"Hold up," he says, pulling her back. "We can't go any closer without risking too much exposure."

They peer around the corner into an empty room where a large mass of cooled lava sits. The mass is many meters in width and length. More is frozen on the ceiling and walls.

Loyola scans the mass with her detector. 5000-year-old decay.

Largoto points his device to the large mass. "I'm getting large amounts of radiation coming from that thing. Enough to permeate through our suits and do real damage. We're risking enough as it is. We need to go."

They emerge from the abyss of Chernobyl.

"You happy now?" says Largoto, agitated. "Exposed us to radiation, but at least you know."

She stomps in front of him. "The radiation of the mass is 5000 years decayed. Not 3000 years of decay. They survived the first nuclear attack, maybe they survived another."

"Fine. We'll do one last fly through, but if we don't see anything, we're done."

The craft glides close to the ground over the grasslands. Herds of antelope, stallions, and other animals avoid the craft. The water parts as the craft zooms across the ocean. Teams of dolphins travel swiftly beneath the water hunting for food.

The craft shoots upwards into the clouds. A large half-circle structure stands in the distance surrounded by a sea of sand.

"Wait," says Loyola. "What is that?"

As they approach, the structure takes on nautilus design. The lone sands surround the structure.

"It's magnificent," says Largoto. He walks around trying to read the inscriptions. "There are drawings on the side of it. Looks like beings working, a ship going upwards." He continues walking around the structure reading. "They made it," he says in astonishment and glee.

"There are weird numbers and symbols engraved here," Loyola says, standing at the edge of the nautilus. "They continue to the center."

She takes out her device and scans the engravings.

"On July 18, 1969," says the device in a computerized tone. "Mother Earth sent two of her sons to venture into the unknown of space. The men who went to the moon to explore in peace stayed on the moon to rest in peace. These brave men, Neil Armstrong and Edwin Aldrin, know there is no hope for their recovery, but there is hope for mankind in their sacrifice.

"In their exploration, they stirred the people of the world to feel as one. In their sacrifice, they bound more tightly the brotherhood of man. Every human since, who gazed at the moon in the nights after, knew there was a corner of another world that is forever mankind.

"This Nautilus monument stands as a decree to humanity's cooperative nature in the face of disaster. The Nautilus is one of the oldest creatures to survive the earth's oceans. Its spiral design symbolizes humanity's growth, expansion, and renewal of our nomadic roots. Like the primitive humans who first crossed the seas into the unknown, we have ventured into the unknown ocean of space. If you seek the next chapter of human life, it lies above you."

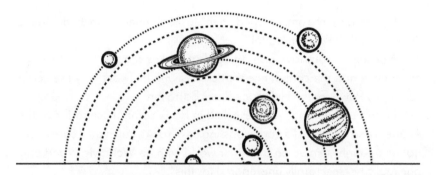

Revelation on Hellscape

By Edward Swing

Junior Lieutenant Tivra Sanyal struggled with the Centurion's jump-thrusters and landed face down on the ground. Though her Academy curriculum had included rudimentary training with jump-capable mechs and she'd mastered basic Centurion operations, Tivra had been floundering for hours.

She pushed up from the machine's latest belly-flop. Broken branches, dirt, and leaves stuck to the chest of her fifteen-meter tall Centurion. She brushed them away with the hands of the colossal mech.

Major Dhona Hopkins insisted on a thorough regimen of drills in the alien wilderness and challenged Tivra with increasingly difficult tests.

"All right, Junior Sanyal," Hopkins said. "It's time for a break. Power down and grab a snack."

Obediently, Tivra climbed out of her cockpit in the Centurion's head, climbed down its arm, and trudged toward her senior partner.

Hopkins offered a tray containing a chicken wrap and a cup of apple slices. Tivra accepted it, grateful the tray contained recognizable foodstuffs. She shuffled her feet and stared at the ground, trying to ignore the golden-colored vegetation surrounding them.

"Cheer up, Tivra. This is your first posting, and you're learning quickly." Hopkins sat on her Bradamante's foot to eat her meal.

"If you say so, ma'am. I tripped on the last drill when I launched. Maybe I'm not Knight's Pawn material."

"Nonsense. You have everything that makes a good Knight except experience and the confidence that comes with it. That's why I selected you as my Pawn for the Hellscape Black Battalion."

"I don't understand why. I excelled in Rook combat scenarios at the Academy, so I thought I'd earn a posting as a Rook's Pawn on a core world, not as a Knight's Pawn on a frontier world with no WorldMesh and only one real city. I feel totally unprepared for this."

Hopkins stood and strolled to one of the trees Tivra had flattened in a fall. She examined the golden leaves and the reddish flowers and fruit. "This world, Hellscape, can be a paradise. It has a perfect climate for humans, and the untamed wilderness offers many opportunities for exploring."

Tivra glanced around at the alien vegetation. Crimson fruits and flowers grew on bushes and trees, each bearing leaves in differing shades of yellowish gold. The high-pitched whistles and droning buzz of the local wildlife reverberated in her ears. Tivra shuddered.

"We can even eat some of the local fruits and creatures," Hopkins continued. She plucked a fruit from the fallen tree, peered at it, then hurled it away. "But not that one. The last two times I tried one of those, it gave me stomach cramps."

Her superior officer flashed a smile. Tivra forced a grin to her face.

"This world seems so strange," Tivra remarked. "The non-Terran life bewilders me."

"You grew up on Venus, right?"

Tivra nodded. "My father ran a terraforming monitor station near Evaki."

"Do these jungles remind you of Venus?"

Tivra recalled her childhood home. "A little. But the early terraformers imported the plants and animals from Earth. The plants were green, not gold, and the animals were normal instead of the weird octopus-things that live here."

"Six legs, not eight," Hopkins corrected. She hurled another fruit into the brush. "My former Pawn couldn't handle this world."

"Why not?" Tivra asked. "Dangerous creatures?"

"No. Some of the local vegetation secretes an enzyme. It doesn't affect most people, but a few have a nasty reaction. Chaiss was one of the unfortunates."

"That's why I had to be tested before transferring here," Tivra recalled. "The Academy administered a bunch of compatibility tests before we accepted our commissions. Did Chaiss die from this enzyme?"

"No, it doesn't kill, but the enzyme caused her to tremble and sweat like a fountain. I had contacts from my tour on Cinone, so she transferred to the White Battalion."

Hopkins gestured at the empty food trays, and Tivra gathered the trash from their snack. The senior stood and climbed the lift-ladder to her Bradamante's cockpit. "Break is over, Sanyal. I want two more hours of drills from you."

Tivra stowed the trash in her Centurion's storage. "May I ask why, ma'am?"

"I'd stretch this training another week, but we have a mission in two days."

"A mission, ma'am?" Tivra gaped.

Excitement crept into Hopkins's voice. "That's right. We'll be escorting a engineering team. They're clearing a path for a roadway from Tenarus to Curtius. Once we transport building materials and supplies to Curtius, NuWorld can develop a second teletranser, and Stardream Enterprises can launch WorldMesh satellites."

"But Curtius is thousands of kilometers away," Tivra replied.

"That's right. Our battalion will send lift-strikers to check on us and bring fresh supplies. We have an opportunity to explore this world!" Hopkins couldn't keep the enthusiastic grin off her face. "It'll be so much fun!"

Tivra gazed at the daunting alien vegetation and tried to muster a veneer of enthusiasm. "Yes, ma'am."

―――――――

Two days later, Tivra followed Major Hopkins on their overland trek. They left Fort Kimaris at dawn, marched through the nearby lands the settlers had cleared for farming, and plunged into Hellscape's thick golden jungle. Hopkins coordinated with the engineering team as they plowed through trees and underbrush, following a route identified by reconnaissance aircraft and creating a wide path a second team could transform into a roadway.

They slowly climbed a rising plateau as they marched eastward. The plateau overlooked a wide swampy valley to the south; Tivra guessed it had been a river canyon before Hellscape's rampant vegetation and humid climate covered the landscape.

After hiking several hours, the team reached a site where the vegetation thinned, and Hopkins called a halt to their trek. "This looks like a good place for first-lunch," she announced. "Let's power down and stretch our human legs. My long-range sensors detect a low-pressure cell coming our way. Let's eat before it drenches us."

Tivra opened her cockpit and scanned the alien jungle, spotting native animals moving in the trees. Before climbing out of her Centurion, she retrieved her las-pistol. The familiar weight of her sidearm eased her anxieties.

The engineering team parked their mechs. Unlike her Centurion or Hopkins's Bradamante, the worker mechs used older technology and lacked a fully humanoid form. She examined the digging apparatus of the excavator mech and the variable assembly of the grader mech, which could convert from short legs to a tracked drive. She marveled at the enormous duronite saw-arm and oversized grasping claw of the timber mech.

Behind the mechs, the team parked their maintenance truck, the milling truck, and the trailer containing bunks, a camp kitchen, and emergency medical supplies.

Tivra followed Hopkins and lined up behind the team at the trailer. The engineering team's leader, an older dark-skinned man Tivra knew as Mr. Bakika, passed out prepared lunches and iced tea brewed from a local plant. Tivra accepted her meal and sat in the shade between the legs of her crouching Centurion.

Hopkins handed her two empty bottles and a water filtration system. "Sanyal, please refill the water supply. I spotted a small creek a quarter kilometer to the north."

Tivra gulped. "Is it safe? What if a wild animal attacks?"

"Our surveys of this area revealed no large predators, and you have your las-pistol," Hopkins replied, glancing at the weapon on Tivra's hip. "But I'll ask one of the surveyors to join you, if you want help."

Hoping to appear professional, Tivra brushed the pollen out of her black hair and straightened her uniform. "Yes, ma'am. I would appreciate the company."

Tivra and a young engineer named Andere navigated through the dense underbrush and reached the creek. They were waiting for the filtration system to finish purifying the water when Tivra noticed movement out of the corner of her eye.

"Shh," Andere hissed. "I see a bevy of pillats. Don't make any sudden moves." He pointed at a group of five creatures descending from the trees to drink. Each resembled an octopus with six legs. The tentacle-like legs, each about ten centimeters long, lifted their bodies off the ground, and their skin resembled brown velour.

The pillats extended their mouths—or some type of feeding tube protruding from their underside—into the water to drink. Between gulps, the creatures trilled a chirping buzz.

Centered on top of their bodies, one large greenish eye gazed around their surroundings and the treetops. Three smaller eyes, radially arranged around the creature's body, scanned the nearby vegetation. One pillat met her gaze and scrambled toward her. Tivra froze in place, and it returned to its fellows.

Tivra sigh of relief transformed into a frightened shriek when a larger creature pounced on the pillat from the underbrush. Twice the size of the small brown creatures, this beast was covered with short golden fur and possessed the same body structure as the pillats. It seized its hapless prey with sharp barbs protruding from the underside of each muscled limb. When its mouth pierced the flesh of the pillat, black blood spurted onto nearby leaves.

The unfortunate animal bleated a final loud buzz then stopped moving. Tivra drew her las-pistol, but the predator ignored her and continued its feast. Tivra's lunch heaved into her throat and spilled onto the ground.

"Are you okay, Junior Sanyal?" Andere asked.

Tivra wiped her mouth and nodded. "Let's hurry back to the others."

The pouring rain slowed progress, but Tivra plodded on, following her superior. When the team stopped again for the second of three midday meals, Tivra ate inside her cockpit to avoid the steady rain.

The group forded a small creek engorged by the rain, and Hopkins scanned the thick vegetation ahead. "Your Centurion is lighter and smaller than my Bradamante. You take the lead."

"Is it safe?" Tivra peered into the dense jungle canopy.

"The most dangerous thing you might find is a deep mud puddle. Follow the map coordinates and you should be fine."

"Yes, ma'am." Tivra pushed her way into the jungle. Following Hopkins' example, she tested the trees, snapping the weakest ones as she probed the foliage. Occasionally, she'd fire the zeta pulsers in her left forearm to break up thick clumps of vegetation. Behind her, the survey team inspected the path she created, and the excavation mech dug up roots and brush, while the grader mech flattened the path for the tracked trucks to follow. In dry weather, a milling truck would cut the trunks into usable lumber, but Mr. Bakika worried about flooding the finicky machinery.

Tivra pressed through the dense jungle for another hour before Hopkins signaled to her.

"Tivra, drop back half kilometer," Hopkins called. "Bakika thinks the ground has gotten too soft for the grader. We'll take another route to the north."

Tivra glanced down at her Centurion's massive feet. Mud and trampled vegetation reached past her ankles. "I agree." She turned to face the engineering team, but as she strode toward the other mechs, her right foot sank into a deep mud hole. She tried to pull free but succeeded in sinking further. "Major Hopkins! I'm stuck!"

"Use your jump-thrusters," Hopkins advised.

Tivra fired her jump-thrusters. The powerful engines pushed her Centurion skyward, but her right foot caught, pausing the ascent. When it broke free, she soared above the treetops.

Disoriented, Tivra rocketed toward the valley.

"Tivra! Balance and counterthrust!" Hopkins yelled. "Keep away from the edge!"

Tivra drew upon her extensive gymnastic conditioning and Academy training to regain her balance in midair. A glance under her feet revealed the approaching drop. She fired her thrusters to stop the lateral motion.

144

The massive Centurion descended to the ground, and Tivra found a clear patch of ground ten meters from the cliff. As the massive mech landed, she relaxed.

Then the ground under her feet dropped away.

Sliding and tumbling with the mudslide down the slope, Tivra tucked into a tight roll. She lost her grip on the Centurion's hand-held railgun, and its arm clasp tore away from her forearm. After several confusing minutes, she landed on the valley floor, along with several tons of mud.

Tivra extricated herself from the tangle of jungle foliage and stood. She spotted the barrel of her railgun poking out of a pile of mud-covered vegetation. She dug it out with her mech's hands, but once unearthed, she discovered the fall had damaged her weapon.

"Junior Sanyal! Tivra! Are you hurt?" Major Hopkins called over the lascom.

Tivra looked up. Silhouetted against the cloudy sky, Hopkins' Bradamante waved at her from the edge.

"I'm okay, ma'am. But my railgun's barrel extender twisted in the fall, and the arm brace sheared off. It's inoperative."

"How is your Centurion? Are your jump-thrusters operational?"

Tivra tried her jump-thrusters, but they didn't fire. She hopped in place. Embarrassed, she initiated a diagnostic analysis.

Alert: Left jump-thruster impaired. Alert: Main gun unavailable. Alert: Minor damage to left shoulder articulators.

Wonderful. Less than a month after graduation and I've broken my first Centurion.

She echoed her status to Hopkins. "I'm afraid I can't climb back up to you. What do I do?"

"Even if your jump-thrusters worked, you couldn't climb this mess. You'd collapse more of the scarp if you tried," Hopkins replied. "Let me check the topological survey."

Two minutes passed. "Sanyal, according to the survey, the ground becomes rocky to the northeast and the valley rises. You should find a place to climb up. It's close to our original path."

"How far, ma'am?"

"About a hundred kilometers. I'm transmitting the coordinates and recommended paths to you now," Hopkins replied. "We both have challenging terrain to navigate. I doubt we'll reach the meeting point before nightfall, so find a good place to camp."

"What about going back?" Tivra asked, then regretted her question. *Will Major Hopkins think I'm trying to run away?*

Her superior gave no hint of disapproval. "I checked, Tivra. The marsh broadens into a wide lake to the southwest."

Tivra's shoulders slumped.

"You excelled in the survival training at the Academy," Hopkins reminded her. "You can handle this, Junior Sanyal."

Tivra stared at the forbidding marshy plants around her. "I don't have a choice, do I?"

"I need to return to the engineering team. Shift to radio frequencies and contact me if you encounter trouble. Move out."

"Yes, ma'am." Tivra scanned the surrounding vegetation and reviewed the recommended paths. Hopkins had plotted three routes through the marsh. Tivra selected the northern course. Though Hopkins and the engineering team couldn't reach her, she took some comfort that the route would keep her close to them.

Hours of slogging through knotted swampy vegetation later, Tivra reached drier ground. Waist-high flowering trees filled a patch of land between the river that fed the marsh and the sheer rise to the ridge above.

She considered sleeping in her Centurion's cramped cockpit overnight but doubted she could get comfortable. Instead, she explored the region and discovered a clearing against the rock wall beside a creek. The small area could fit the Centurion and her enviro-tent, so Tivra stopped for the night. Before powering down, she reported her status to Major Hopkins.

She lowered the Centurion to kneel on one knee, clipped her las-pistol to her hip, and climbed out of the cockpit. Standing on the Centurion's shoulder, she gazed across the marshy valley. The combination of the golden leaves and crimson flowers evoked an image of a field on fire.

Perhaps that's why the early settlers called this world Hellscape.

Tivra deploying her enviro-tent and examined the Centurion's jump-thrusters. She brushed away the dried mud that covered the right thruster, verifying it had no damage. The fall had somehow wedged an entire bush in the left thruster, complete with an extensive root system and huge clumps of mud. Grunting and swearing, Tivra extricated the tangled mess. Wishing she had the power washer in the mech hangar, she scrubbed the interior of the thruster and realigned it.

By the time Hellscape's sun began to set, Tivra had purified a bottle of water from the nearby river and eaten an early dinner from her prepared meals. Despite the warm evening, she built a small campfire from twigs and branches the Centurion had snapped when it entered the clearing. After she cleaned her meal, she sat at the campfire and tried to relax.

The buzzing and hooting of local wildlife echoed throughout the valley, and Tivra's hand sought the comforting grip of her las-pistol. Some of the local wildlife roamed among the trees, seeking food. Twice, small creatures emerged from the nearby trees and approached her. The eerie reflection of the firelight in their central eye terrified her. When she seized a stick from the fire, they scurried back into the trees.

The sky darkened, and the leaves on nearby trees began to glow a fiery orange. Even the leaves on the fallen branches emitted a faint glow. Fascinated, Tivra plucked a few leaves, ignoring the tiny arboreal creatures the size of her hand hopping up the branches to the treetops.

I guess I won't need a fire, after all. I wonder why they glow.

While she examined a glowing bush, a series of buzzes and hoots erupted behind her. She whirled, expecting another local creature to have approached the fire, and she gasped at what she saw.

Two creatures peered into the fire with their strange eyes, and twenty more climbed onto her Centurion to explore its surface. Three reached the mech's head while one hung from the top of the railgun. Another perched on the cluster-rocket launcher on its left shoulder and probed the launch tube with its tentacles.

Like other life-forms native to Hellscape, the creatures vaguely resembled a six-legged octopus. But these creatures walked on four half-meter limbs, and two adjacent limbs were longer, branching into four fingerlike tendrils near their tip. Three smaller eyes accompanied the creature's large yellow eye on the center of its body, but instead of the radial arrangement of other creatures she'd seen on Hellscape, the small eyes spanned the gap between the longer tentacle-arms. She couldn't discern the location of the creature's mouth but assumed it extended from their underside.

"Stop it! Go away!" she yelled and bolted to the fire to seize a flaming stick. The creatures near the firepit climbed on top of her enviro-tent while hooting to their fellows. The others responded with a bizarre chorus of hoots and buzzes.

"Get off my Centurion!" Tivra swung her impromptu torch at the creatures, but they climbed higher on its huge frame. She activated the lift-ladder; as it raised her to the mech's shoulder, the creatures moved away but continued to explore the giant mech.

A shifting light distracted her from her ineffective pursuit. From her perch on the Centurion's shoulder, she noticed one of the creatures had returned to the firepit; it was waving a burning stick in the air with awkward motions.

"No! You could hurt yourself!" Tivra reversed the lift-ladder and descended to the ground. She rushed toward the fire, but the creature, distracted by its prize, failed to notice her until she grabbed the burning stick.

"Let's put this back in the firepit." She tried to force the creature to return the stick to the fire, but it wriggled the stick in her grasp, and she had to release it.

"Okay, let's try it this way." Tivra sat by the fire again and returned her own burning branch to the pit. Then she found a nearby twig and added it to the firepit. She continued adding more wood, and the blaze brightened.

Eventually, the creature dropped its stick into the pit and added two more. It buzzed and whooped, and another creature joined it. Together, they continued to throw sticks into the fire until the excess began to choke the flames.

Tivra held her hand over the fire. "That's enough," she announced.

The creatures ignored her and continued to add wood until they extinguished the flame. This started another cycle of hoots and buzzes.

Maybe they're like monkeys, imitating what I do. They don't seem dangerous after all, just curious.

She activated her wristlet-comm to record the antics and watched them explore the Centurion until fatigue overcame her fascination. Stifling a series of yawns, she doused the firepit with water, opened her enviro-tent, and climbed inside. One creature tried to follow her, and she had to shoo it away. After sealing the tent, she lay down and placed her las-pistol near her head. Despite the cacophony outside, she fell into a deep slumber.

The noise outside her tent had vanished by the time Tivra woke the next morning. She ate a quick breakfast and steeled herself for another encounter with the strange creatures. Expecting another horde of the curious natives climbing on her mech or perhaps finding them asleep, she stepped out of her tent.

Only one creature remained in the clearing, and it buzzed at her, demanding attention. Beside it, looming three meters tall, a humanoid figure built from sticks, leaves, and flowers kneeled on one knee. The figure held a long stick in its right hand, and a boxy shape fashioned from a bush sat on its left shoulder.

"What the—" Tivra glanced at her Centurion and gasped. "By the stars! It's in the same pose!"

She circled the strange monument, her jaw agape. The long stick, mirroring her railgun, tilted at the same angle, and a roughly circular depression in the boxy bush matched the launch tube for her cluster-rocket launcher.

Still shocked, she turned to the remaining creature. "Did you make this?"

The creature responded with a hoot followed by a long, low buzz.

Captivated by the handiwork, realization dawned on her. *These creatures are sapient!*

Tivra would have stared at the strange effigy for an hour, but hooting from the tent startled her. Inside, the creature had buried itself under her blanket, and its longer tentacles were exploring her camp-pack. It uttered a series of sharp whistling hoots when it noticed her peering at it.

"Are you proud of yourself? Go back outside," Tivra urged. The creature continued its exploration.

I should record this, she remembered. She activated her wristlet-comm and recorded a holo-rec of the creature as it explored. Then she recorded a detailed image of the large figure the creatures had built, including a reference image of her Centurion.

By the time she finished, the creature had crawled out of her tent, carrying her blanket in its tentacles. It hooted at her again.

Tivra considered letting the curious creature keep the blanket, but worried something in the blanket might poison it. She snatched it from the creature, eliciting a loud buzz.

"I'm sorry. I can't let you keep it." She knelt next to the creature and used her wristlet-comm to display the holo-recording of exploring her tent. It whistled, then tried to touch its image. A fingered tentacle passed through the hologram and brushed her arm.

Tivra froze as it touched her arm and shoulder, but she flinched away when it tried to touch her face. "That will have to be enough," she announced.

She retrieved her camp-pack and signaled the enviro-tent to fold itself into a compact rectangular mound. Striking camp, the creature followed her during the entire process.

"I'm afraid I have to leave," she told the creature. "But I'll come back some day."

After verifying that none of the creatures were lingering on the Centurion, she hopped onto the lift-ladder and climbed into her cockpit. Tivra clipped the cere-link onto her head and initiated the connection to her Centurion.

The colossal mech surged to life. Keeping an eye on the creature below, she grabbed the folded tent with the Centurion's left hand, opened the storage compartment in her thigh, and dropped the tent inside.

The creature capered around her feet, hooting and buzzing. Now linked to the Centurion's sensors, she spotted the rest of its tribe watching from the trees. She stepped back and watched as the rest of bizarre creatures returned to the clearing and joined in the strange dance.

Tivra took one giant step over the creatures, then another. She took one final look at them and continued her trek through the alien rainforest.

After three hours, Tivra reached a place where craggy boulders replaced the muddy escarpment. She scanned the rise with the Centurion's sensors and identified a path to the plateau above.

Before she started her climb, she tested her jump-thrusters with a series of short hops.

"Major Hopkins, I've arrived at the rendezvous point. I've repaired my jump-thrusters, and I'm starting my ascent now."

"Confirmed. We're approaching your position," Hopkins replied. "Proceed at your discretion."

Firing her jump-thrusters with careful bursts, Tivra hopped from one huge boulder to another. Balancing on one foot, she relied on her gymnastics training as she leapt between boulders. After a harrowing climb, she reached the top.

Hopkins's Bradamante reached out to steady her. "Good job, Sanyal. You can rest now; the engineering team prepared first-lunch for you."

"Thank you, ma'am." Tivra followed her senior partner to the circle of engineering mechs and men. A savory aroma greeted her as she opened the Centurion's cockpit. Beside her, Major Hopkins deactivated her Bradamante and descended to the ground.

She circled the Centurion while Tivra climbed down. Staring at the mud caked on the Centurion's armor, she announced, "You'll clean that off when we return to Fort Kimaris."

Tivra flushed with embarrassment. "Yes, ma'am."

"Relax, Junior Sanyal. Let's get something to eat."

"Yes, ma'am." But before Tivra joined the group, she walked to the edge of the plateau and gazed down into the marshy valley, focusing on the distant copse of trees where she had camped.

Soft footsteps sounded behind her. Major Hopkins followed her gaze. "I assume your trek was uneventful, Tivra?"

Tivra turned to face her commander. "No, ma'am. I had quite an adventure." The hesitancy vanished, and words spilled out of her mouth as she recounted the encounter with the strange creatures, their fascination with her Centurion, and the uncanny monument they created.

"You believe these creatures are intelligent?" Hopkins asked once she finished her tale.

"Yes, ma'am. I couldn't decide whether they saw the Centurion as a divine being or a strange visitor, but their actions exceeded anything an animal might do. They scared me at first, but I think they found me as fascinating as I found them."

"I'll notify the planetary officials and request they send a first-contact team to the valley. Would you want to join them?"

Tivra hesitated, then nodded. "Yes, ma'am."

Hopkins smiled. "Now you understand why I chose you as my Pawn? The Rook Team focuses on close combat, and the Bishop Team excels with ranged weaponry. But the Knight Team, which fills the role of scouts, experiences things the other teams could only dream of."

Tivra turned around to stare at the Bradamante and Centurion, both crouched over the circle of engineers. "You selected me because you wanted to share these experiences with me?"

The Major nodded. "Several of your instructors at the Academy commended your ability to adapt to unexpected situations. They recommended you for a posting where you'd face a variety of challenges. As a Knight's Pawn, and eventually as a Knight, you can explore them."

"I didn't realize a Knight's position had so much to do," Tivra replied in a small voice.

"On most worlds, they don't." Hopkins replied, laughing. "But on the frontier, a Knight has the best job in the company."

Tivra faced the valley again, recalling her encounter. "Then I look forward to our next adventure."

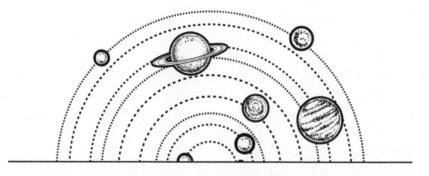

Co-Creation

By Judy Backhouse

"If you really want to hear about it, you'll need a hundred of my sol-orbits. Do you have that much time?"

"Actually, I do."

"Hmmmf." A dust cloud arose on one of my larger planes and swirled across the surface. "You're a small species, so I was guessing short-lived."

"Yes, short-lived, but with cool mods, both biological and technological, that put me on your time-scale. If I understand your time-scale correctly."

The small creature added this qualifier with modest self-deprecation, which pleased me. Feeling about in my substrates, I could sense the metal and bio compounds it was constructed of. I sensed tensions between the precise logic of circuitry and the broad intuition of wet-ware. It felt and looked messy. Cobbled together without the precise design of evolved biological forms. The strangest thing I'd encountered in my twenty galaxy-orbits.

Skeptical and a little tired, I wasn't about to launch into a local history lesson without good cause. "Why do you want to know? Where are you from?"

"I come from a planet orbiting a star in the Tucana III dwarf galaxy, not so far from your Milky Way."

I tried to place Tucana III. I knew the name, like one knows a distant city or country, and tried to sense a direction and distance, but my knowledge was too vague.

It waited quietly for my response, and I began to feel in it a sizable reserve of patience. Patience is rare in this universe, particularly in smaller species. I probed the edges of that patience, first sharing nothing, a slight hint of warmth, then cool disinterest. The creature remained calm and open. Patient.

"Why do you want to know?"

"Well, um, because I am interested in your history."

"The history of Sol? Out of all the stars?"

"Yes, the history of Sol and your siblings. You are a pretty unique family."

I was still skeptical, but I'd heard of galaxy-roving scholars. Perhaps this was one of them. "How long have you got?"

"Well," it paused, "I think about three hundred of your sol-orbits, if I've understood those correctly."

"You know how long a sol-orbit is?"

"Oh, yes."

It sounded ridiculously confident. I asked, "And you know all our sol-orbits are different, right?"

"I get that, but talking in galaxy-orbits is hard for me. That scale is beyond the boundaries of my constructs. I figured I'd have to work in sol-orbits and adjust for whoever I'm talking to."

"How do you measure time where you come from?"

"It's species-dependent. We have an ancient system unrelated to the orbits of our planet and star, but we've stuck to it."

"Different time measures on the same planet? That must be confusing."

"It happens. You get used to it."

This weird little creature seemed rather well-informed about sol and my siblings. I sensed a lot of preparation had gone into this visit. It made me curious. We don't often get visitors of a sentient nature, and when we do, they are largely ignorant. Perhaps it would be worth the effort, after all. It's not like I had much else to think about.

"Very well. I'll tell you what I know."

Respectful silence was the only acknowledgement.

"It was about four galaxy-orbits back, four and a half, although it feels closer. Things were simpler then. Fewer travelers, quiet orbits, not much happened in our corner of the galaxy..."

"My sister, Ethar. She's the one that suffered the most.

"Me, I never had the parasites. Wasn't forced to live with them. I could just change slowly, at my own pace. Focus on my own thoughts, respond to sensations and emotions as they arose. I shifted layers, shed layers. Rock creaking across rock. Dry red sand flowing into the gaps, warm and comforting. A little water and ice, occasional eruptions of gas. But never parasitical life forms, just my own substrates, my own substance.

"Ethar experimented with lifeforms. You know, she has oceans. They were blue, back then. Quite the poet, Ethar was. She's the only one of us that could say blue and get it right—exactly a nuanced combination of boundless calm, deep melancholy and a sprinkling of delight."

The creature jolted me from my literary ruminations.

"About the lifeforms. You were saying?"

"Oh yes. Ethar started slowly, with sea-plants in her oceans, then tried growing them out of the water. Refined the plants until she had trees. Magnificent things those, tall and green. She spread them across her surface in a display of aspirational yearning, determined hard work, and sheer joy. Green on blue." I caught myself beginning to drift again. "That was pretty much it for the first two, nearly three galaxy orbits.

"Then she got carried away. Made independent creatures not rooted to her substance. Some of them crawled along her surface, some could fly in her atmosphere. Ugh! It makes my crust crawl, just to think of it. She experimented with how they moved. Wings and legs. Tried eight legs, six legs, four legs. Obsessed with symmetry, she was. Legs and wings had to come in pairs.

"Finally, she made people. Curious little bipeds. They were supposed to be intelligent, so she said. She called them sentient, as though they were like us. I think she was hoping to communicate with them, establish some kind of mutualism. But they were tiny. Miniatures if you like. Things on that scale have little to offer a planet. It's not like there was a clear symbiotic benefit. I mean, what could short-lived creatures with puny bodies do for a planet?

"Ethar calls me a scale-bigot. I guess she's right. I don't have a lot of time for creatures on very different scales. So alien."

How bizarre anything should be considered living, when it appeared and disappeared in the time it took me to hold a conversation. Then, remembering my small listener, I felt a hint of embarrassment. It gave no sign of offense. The feelings were calm and open. Patient.

"As I was saying, Ethar got overrun with these 'people'. Tens of billions, in the end. They made a real mess. Not that they could seriously threaten her lovely rounded form, her consciousness, but they did change the contours of her continents and wiped out many of the pretty life forms she'd accumulated.

"Mostly, the damage was psychological. She was a maker, you know. Liked to shape new lifeforms, just for the joy of seeing the abundance. She'd set up a complex environment for them too. Oceans with powerful currents and a swirling atmosphere. Continents for the crawling lifeforms. Took a lot of trouble over these refinements. Many of us couldn't really understand why. The whole project took her four galaxy-orbits. That's a substantial part of our lifetime.

"You can imagine how heartbroken she was when her little proteges destroyed it. Absolutely no respect for what she'd done. It didn't help they were supposed to be the pinnacle of her creations, the sentient ones, if you could call it that. They certainly had the capacity to sense and feel, but for some reason, they imagined they were unique in this. Never considered the rest of Ethar's creations might also be sentient, never mind Ethar herself.

"So, what happened?" the small, compound creature from Tucana III interrupted.

I was contemplating the philosophical distinction between sentience and sapience, the sensing and feeling qualities contrasted with thinking, with wisdom. Feelings are excellent indicators as to which direction to take. They give uncomplicated signals of what is working and what is not. Thinking and wisdom, however, are much harder. Employing them effectively is beyond the capacity of most creatures, certainly beyond the little, wet species Ethar had made.

"Hmm. What happened?" A long pause while I gathered my thoughts. "Now, where was I?"

"You were telling me about your sister and her, um, parasites. They were destructive?"

"You could say that. Called themselves sapient, as though they were wise, but did not have the wisdom to understand the complex, interconnected system Ethar had put together. Took them almost their entire evolutionary trajectory to forget what they knew about interdependence; such was the warping effect of their prized binary logic. By the time they got back to understanding, it was too late. The surface system was wildly unstable."

"Bummer. What she made seems really interesting. Rich, abundant, inventive. I'd like to have seen it."

"Yes, it was all those things. I mean, I never got to see her people close-up, but watching her pass by in her orbit was a delight. She shone. Blue, green, a smattering of yellow-brown and white. You could see from ten light-years away she was doing something special."

"Your other siblings haven't tried anything like that?"

"No, not even close. I mean, Nartus has those colorful rings, but that's decorative. Nothing living. And Prijuet loves playing with color and collecting moons. Such a show-off. Nothing like Ethar."

"I hear you had your own experiments with water."

Impudent stranger. I did not want to talk about my own attempts to shape my surface with water. That was a long time back, when I was very young, and it didn't work out the way I'd hoped. I responded with a stony glare. One sol-orbit. Two sol-orbits. Three sol-orbits.

Then it spoke again, "So, what happened to Ethar's parasites?"

I waited for half a sol-orbit before responding. I didn't want it to think I was sulking.

"Well, she kept hoping they would figure it out, that their intelligence would lead to more harmonious ways of living. Some of them tried, but they never seemed to learn how to work together, collectively. Laughable, really. For such a swarm of creatures, they had a rudimentary sense of themselves as a whole species. Always fighting against each other. Some kind of self-destructive streak.

"In the end, Ethar admitted defeat and shrugged them off. They were that uncomfortable. She allowed dense clouds to build up in the atmosphere, creating a dark hot-box. Heated up her surface, making it more difficult for them to grow food, find water, all the things they needed. They stopped reproducing and their numbers dwindled. Many died. I think it was very hard on her, having to destroy what she'd made. It took a hundred of her sol-orbits, but eventually there were none left."

"And once they were gone?"

"She gave up. Stopped stirring her oceans. Let them stagnate. Sank into depression. If you look at her now, she's grey and listless. She still follows her orbit, turns on her axis as she always did, but she's lost her glow. Composes morbid poetry, that sort of thing, for the last million or so of my sol-orbits."

"A sorry tale, sir."

I stared off into the distant heart of the galaxy. It was painful to remember what Ethar had been and how she had changed.

"None survived?" it asked.

"None of the people, none of the moving creatures, none of the trees."

"None?"

The question stirred a faint memory. "Actually, I suppose some people might have."

"What makes you think so?"

"Towards the end, a few developed technologies that kept them alive off-surface. I mean, outside of Ethar's atmosphere. They started sending little machines out beyond her skies. Even, at one stage, to my surface."

"But you never had parasites?"

"No, no, there were no people in those machines. They were electrical machines, but not sentient in any way. It lasted twenty or thirty of my sol-orbits. They would descend and lie about on my surface. Some discharged even smaller machines that could crawl, but so tiny they were hard to notice. I was annoyed, but I tolerated them to humor Ethar. I did bury a few under dust storms. I'd quite forgotten about that.

"Some of them went to our sister Evuns. She had a bit more trouble but got rid of them in the end."

"Didn't you say the people were kept alive? I may have misheard."

"Oh, yes. What I mean is, some of the machines, the ones that stayed closer to Ethar, had people in them. I think at some stage people went to her moon.

"Anyway, the point is, towards the end when she was being destructive, some of those machines left Ethar. I've just realized there may have been people in them."

———————————

Sometime later, I became aware my listener was still there, still listening.

"Can I ask you something?" I said.

"Sure, sir, not that I have a fraction of your wisdom to share."

"I've been thinking about this, about Ethar. Around here, she was the only one. You know, the only one of us to try anything like that. Like I said, we have Nartus and Prijuet with their trinkets and trophies, but mostly, my kind stick to their non-living cores. Some experiment with atmospheres, various chemical compounds, some are gaseous, but most are content to remain as solid and uniform as possible. It's easier that way. I've scanned the cosmos looking for something like Ethar, but I haven't sensed a thing. Nothing.

"I wanted to ask you, since you have travelled, have you encountered planets like Ethar? Truly creative planets?"

There was a respectful silence for a few sol-orbits. The small creature was thinking carefully or, more likely, was trying to give the impression it was taking my question seriously.

"Um." Another pause. "Yes. Yes, I have."

"Tell me about it."

"Well, I've travelled a bit. Not only this trip to the main galaxy, but before that, to small galaxies near my home. I can think of three planets that showed signs of being creative.

"One of them, over in Grus I, flourished about three galactic years, like Ethar, is no longer making. Another, in Pegasus III, is thriving, although in a different direction. Silicon-based life forms there, lots of them. Also obsessed with symmetry, he is. Rotational, transformational, many-faceted. In many dimensions, too. All the creations, from dust speck-sized to planet-stomping monsters, have beautiful symmetries. Lots of light too. Everything glows."

"And the third one?"

"That's the newest. That's where I'm from, near Tucana Three."

"How lucky to encounter three in your short lifespan."

"Well, I'm more mobile than you. No family ties. No obligations to stay in orbit."

"Yes. You are not one of us." My thoughts drifted off, wondering what it would be like to be untethered. To be able to travel and explore. To live without the constant, stabilizing pull of a parent star.

The creature waited until my thoughts circled back to it.

"Tell me about your home," I said.

"It's a minor planet in a large family, twenty of them, on the outer edges of Tucana III. We call it Etharian. Etharian orbits with a twin, Otherian, but she's always on the other side of our star. Etharian has nine apex species, of which we are the newest."

"You are a new species?"

"New to Etharian. We've been there less than a million of your sol-orbits, but the other species were established when we arrived. Also, we were quite different then."

"Different how?"

"Well, um, more flesh, less tech."

A horrible sensation was shifting under my dusty, ruddy surface. I felt itchy, irritated. I thought back to Ethar's people. To those little tin cans emerging from her clouds and travelling towards the more distant members of the family. They could not have had much in the way of resources in those rudimentary vessels. If people had been in those machines, I didn't hold out much hope for them.

Some of my distant siblings reported seeing them go past. We monitored them until they left Sol's influence but never heard anything more about them. Was it possible some might have survived?

The feeling stirred again. Recognition? It was something about the smell of the creature. Highly processed compounds and electrical circuits. Maybe the recognition had to do with the structure? A few sealed spaces with a messy tangle of connecting bits trailing around it. Perhaps the vibration? It hummed a little at very high frequencies.

The only thing I'd encountered like this creature were those machines the people had sent to my surface so long ago.

Could this creature be related to Ethar's parasites?

160

"Your measure of time," I said. "Is it similar to any of ours?"

"We call them years. The closest would be Ethar's sol-orbits."

The response was off-hand, but I sensed it was watching me intently.

I spent twelve sol-orbits absorbing this information. Then the questions began to rumble through my mind. If this was a parasite, did I want it here? Was it just passing through? Would it settle on my surface? Go back to Ethar? Hurt her again?

I thought I'd start slowly. "Why are you here?"

"Actually, I'm here to apologize."

The creature was fast. It had been observing my reaction and guessed at my thought process as, during my silence, dust storms of indignation arose, settled, and swirled again. There were several loud cracks as my mantle contracted and expanded angrily. It took me a while to calm down.

Another sol-orbit passed. The small intruder spoke again.

"You are right. I am a descendant. When your sister shrugged the people off, few had mastered movement through space. About four million of them left before the darkness became complete. They took the slow route out of the Sol system, then jumped through several wormholes, looking for a place to settle."

I made no attempt to keep the contempt from my voice. "Like fleas looking for another dog."

"Just like fleas," it agreed. "And like fleas, we weren't welcome. But we found someone, eventually, who would take us on. We've been there two million of our years now."

It paused, watching as I absorbed the news.

"You survived?"

"We survived. We even thrived."

"You improved your technology, too. You are bigger, and more compound, than Ethar's people were."

The creature shrugged. "We learned a lot from the other species. The Almoira have subtle technology. The Lusinites are genius at social systems. Much of this integration was accomplished by the Tocosts. They are good at bio-mechanical and bio-electrical interfaces. And the Chwirs have mastered the longevity of biological systems. That's a great boon. They taught us. We found them generous."

"These other apex species were happy to have another species join them on their minor planet?"

"Yes, they were. They've learned different species results in multiple, varied ways of thinking, new knowledge, and greater advances."

"And apart from your structures, have you changed in ways of being?"

"The old histories told us we had a lot to learn."

"What have you learned?"

"Humility, I guess. Among equally competent species, we couldn't have it all our own way. We had to gain acceptance, learn their ways, learn to co-operate. To share with tolerance and trust. We spent a lot of time learning to listen, observe, and empathize.

"Then we had to learn the relationship between thinking and acting: to think more carefully, deeply, seeking out ideas and perspectives, and only acting more slowly and with less hubris when we had good reason to. To make modest changes and observe closely. We learned to be open to being wrong, again and again. Accepted the idea of never being right. We try not to hold opinions...Oh, there is so much to list, but you know the qualities Ethar's humans lacked. We have become better at sensing and wiser in acting."

"Is that so?" I was skeptical. Two million of Ethar's sol-orbits was one million of my sol-orbits. How much change could have happened in such a short time? But then, they were a fast-lived species. Such species evolve rapidly. And it did have the help of other advanced species. Perhaps that was enough time for significant remaking?

It had certainly proved to be a good listener since taking up orbit around me, some sixty sol-orbits back. It might just be an evolved form of Ethar's wildest experiment.

I turned my face away from Sol, and the creature, to ponder.

"Does Ethar know you are here?"

"She may have sensed it in your reaction just now."

"You haven't approached her?"

"We crept in on this side because we wanted to talk to you first."

"To me? Why?"

"To hear how Ethar's doing. To learn if it's appropriate to approach her. We're assuming she's still mad at us."

"She probably is. At least, not angry, but upset. Probably with herself."

What would Ethar make of these weird mutant descendants of her humans? I really wasn't sure.

For starters, they were ugly. None of those lovely, flesh-covered bipedal forms Ethar had been so proud of. The creature hovering beyond my gravitational pull was a metal junk-yard, welded together with a firm focus on function, and a complete disregard for form.

"Where are your bio components? Do you still have skin?"

"Oh, buried deep. We keep small skin pouches to remind ourselves of touch, but we don't use them anymore."

"Ethar will be disappointed. She was proud of human skin and the sense of touch."

"With good reason. We value it highly and use our skin pouches on sacred occasions."

Far larger than the humans Ethar had dreamt, the creature had several shrunken, fleshy components embedded in the machine-shell construction and connected by electrical circuits. I could sense more than one individual in there, in different parts of the shell, and yet it had a single identity. It spoke with one voice. Some kind of compound human?

"When you say *we*—Am I talking to more than one person?"

"You are. Individualism went out of fashion and compound creatures are more effective. We live in pods of six to ten individuals, some older, some younger. The individuals die and new ones join, but the pod lives on indefinitely. For voyages like this, we like to have at least ten people to cover the skills needed. Once, we would have considered ourselves ten individuals, but now we are one construct, one pod."

"You *have* changed." It was part statement, part question, part musing aloud.

"Oh yes."

"I wonder if it's for the better?"

"We like to think so, but we are interested to hear what Ethar thinks. Since she dreamed up people, only she can be the judge of how we've evolved."

The strange little creature was right. Ethar would be able to judge how it, or rather its kind, had developed.

"What do you think? Should we approach her?"

Loath to answer, I spent a few sol-orbits trying to picture her likely reactions. On one hand, I imagined Ethar might find such a meeting frightening, given how they had parted company. On the other, I could imagine she would be curious, at least, to see how they had turned out. If their purpose really was to apologize and make amends, it might be a way to get her out of her depression. It might give her hope to see her creatures again.

The patient parasite waited for me.

Eventually, I replied, "Approach her and see how she responds."

We exchanged goodbyes, polite expressions of pleasure, and insincere promises to talk again for another ten sol-orbits, then I watched the misshapen thing set off to align with Ethar's orbit. What would Ethar think of it?

––––––––––––

It was difficult to judge what Ethar thought. Communicating in our family is always tricky. We can usually see each other, unless there is something between us, but it takes time to form the thoughts and communicate them. Especially when the topic is something out of the ordinary. I mean, mutant descendants of a parasite species one wants to forget are not an everyday topic. I wasn't sure I'd have the words I needed to get that across.

I was wary of raising the subject with her did, but I did let her know what to expect. Would she be angry? Upset? Curious? Given she's been in a foul mood since their departure, I hoped (secretly, under my mantle) enough of the creator remained alive under her dark clouds to stir her curiosity. She might even be proud of her hideous progeny.

I'd started to compose my communication as soon as I'd figured out the connection, but by the time the creature headed out, Ethar knew something was up.

"There's something coming your way," I said.

"Thanks. Size?"

"Tiny. Less than two-thousandths of your biggest mountain. And ugly."

"What? That's negligible. Why the notice?"

"It's sentient."

"Sentient? I don't like small, sentient things."

I chuckled, a cliff or two collapsing in rumbling stones. "I'm sure you don't. But I think you'll find this one interesting."

A sneering plume of smoke arose from near her equator. "Unlikely."

"Keep an eye out. It's polite—for a small creature."

The cloud on one quadrant lifted like an eyebrow, then closed again, frowning. "I'll keep an eye out."

It took three of my sol-orbits for the creature to move to Ethar. It waited a respectful two of Ethar's sol-orbits, just out of sight and shielded from her view by Sol's light. I think it knew I would warn her. Perhaps it wanted her to have time to digest.

Then it peered out, shifting slowly. I watched it maneuver to an orbit outside of her moon. Keeping its distance.

Ethar was not welcoming. Her clouds blackened and swirled. I expected her to spit lava but, from where I was watching, there was none of that.

For the entire duration of my next sol-orbit, I strained to sense what was going on.

The next time they passed close by me, I asked, "Everything OK?"

"Fine," she replied.

On the next orbit, "Everything OK?"

"Things just got weird."

Another of my sol-orbits, I smiled at Ethar.

"You knew?" she asked, outraged.

"Sure, I did." Ethar blew dust-plumes at me.

Another sol-orbit.

"So, what do you think?" I asked.

"Still processing."

I could see new patterns in her cloud cover. Signs of a conversation. I couldn't follow the details, but there was definitely communication. The small, messy intruder still hung in her orbit. It waved a jagged metal protrusion at me as I passed.

For the next five sol-orbits, Ethar ignored me, absorbed in her own thoughts. The creature was waiting quietly, and I said nothing.

Time passed. I waited.

And waited.

And waited.

The conversation took another twenty of my sol-orbits, closer to forty of Ethar's. But in that time, I observed a change. Her cloud cover was lifting. She was still a dull grey, but lighter than she'd been in years. Gradually, the creature moved closer to her surface.

Then a time came when I could no longer see the ugly metal blob. It appeared to have vanished. I scanned the spaces between the near planets, but nothing. It could only mean Ethar had agreed to a landing. It had taken fifty of her sol-orbits.

———————

I was looking the other way, watching Opulot gyrating madly at the far end of our family home. Opulot had a habit of bounding about, up and down, out of the orbital plane. There'd been some doubt about his level of sentience.

As I turned slowly back, I glimpsed what looked like a swarm of tiny meteors coming in towards Sol from the edge of the galaxy. They were headed towards Ethar. I watched in horror as they surrounded her. For a while I couldn't see Ethar. The swarm obscured my view, but slowly the fuzz around her cleared until a few of the larger objects remained visible. I hadn't seen the rest of them leave. Obviously, they had landed. What was this? An invasion?

I strained to see what was going on. I signaled as fast as I could to Ethar. "What's up? Are you OK?"

It took an anxious half a sol-orbit for her to reply. "It's OK. I invited them."

"You did?" My own Hellas Planitia turned incredulously white for the next half of that sol-orbit.

"I did."

"You aren't afraid that they—that they—"

"It's OK. I think they have changed."

"I hope you are right."

I kept an anxious watch on her as we drifted away from each other.

Several orbits later, as we passed close by, I said, "You are looking good."

It was true. There was a hint of blue about her. Ethar was showing her true colors again.

"Yes," was her simple answer, and she parted her clouds to reveal a smile of ocean.

"How? How can you do this so fast?"

She laughed, revealing a continent shaded green. "Oh, I'm still as slow as ever. It's the humanoids. They're fast. Sometimes a bit too fast for me. But they're doing this."

"And, you are OK with it?"

"Oh, yes." She beamed at me as our paths drew apart again. "They figured it out, you know. Figured out how to sense at a planetary scale, to rely on feelings, to understand the inter-connectedness. This is what I hoped for them all along. They were side-tracked by sapience, by the pursuit of wisdom, but they learned to connect, to use good feelings and bad feelings to direct their activities. They got over their belief in logic."

"And you want to have them back?"

"They have evolved."

I couldn't help but be skeptical. "Is that what they said?"

"Well, you spoke to the first one. You felt the patience, the thoughtfulness. They did their homework.

"Turns out that my big mistake was individuality, and they are hybrid creatures now. They live as groups. It's a clever solution. Helps them to think long-term. I mean, it's a bit like what I tried to do with families, but that didn't always work out. What it means is wide-ranging skills, learning in each pod, and balance. They keep each other in check. No extremes of emotion because they soothe and support each other. No extremes of ego because they can't survive alone."

"An elegant solution. Still, you take a risk."

"You are right. It's risky, but I thought it through. You see, it wasn't just that they asked forgiveness, for a second chance. I realized, they get it. They appreciate the whole thing, my vision.

"They remember so much of what I did. Kept records. The mountains, rivers, lakes, all the beautiful places. The drama of the coastlines. They recorded it all. They also recorded many of the creatures. Not the full size-spectrum, of course. They were narrowly focused on things of a size similar to their own, but they have records of giraffes and the octopuses. Some of the wackiest things I made. I love that they share my sense of humor."

Her clouds lit up, swirling in delicate patterns over her oceans. It felt so good to have her smiling again.

"I always thought they didn't care for it all, but it turns out they did. They came to make amends. Literally. They've been building again. Repairing the damage to my crust, cleaning the atmosphere. They brought back seeds and even DNA samples of other creatures. We have nurseries. As soon as the atmosphere improves, we'll let the little ones out. There are new animals I have plans for. These compound forms; I really like the idea. I'm going to experiment with those.

"Actually, it's useful to start again. A chance to rethink a few things. Flies, for example."

Ethar was glowing.

Her enthusiasm was infectious.

My thoughts drifted to the frozen water just under my crust.

"I wonder..."

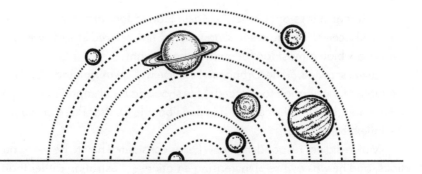

The Ending

By Jim Kent

No one looked up as Makin entered the Celarium. No one spoke a greeting. Each experienced what couldn't be ignored; the sudden onslaught of fierce heat crushed through the briefly opened doorway and the acrid-bitter stench of burning.

"It grows worse," Kale murmured to no one in particular, and no one responded for his utterance was of the inevitable. Most of their world was a smoldering graveyard; scorched, dead, and desolate. Within hours, days at the most, the exploding sun would destroy their dying planet.

Makin, exhausted from his brief foray into the harshness of the outer rooms, collapsed into a chair and stared at the vision-screen dominating the high wall above the consoles. The screen was blank, a nothingness of white except for the occasional electronic flicker fingering across it. The outside cameras, a short time earlier smothered in polar snow, had heat-fused and failed.

His eyes shifted urgently to the smaller screens in the upper console panel.

Lexus anticipated his thoughts. "It remains a good contact," he said. "The Out-Regions Orbitor has not been affected—yet. A decision has to be made. We must hasten."

"You fear a loss of contact?" Makin leaned forward to peer at the Orbitor Receiver, seeing a spiraling mass of tiny colored stars framing a small dark blob almost too far away to be relevant.

Lexus scowled. "The Orbitor will survive us," he murmured, "but will we survive long enough to succeed?" He shook his head impatiently. "The time is now, Makin. The subject is in position, the Orbitor Pulse on target, the Inflext Seeding set."

Makin did not respond. He knew Lexus considered him to be over-cautious, and he was aware of increasing emotions— frustration rather than anger. He shifted his chair towards the main console, motioning impatiently for Drark to move aside.

Drark was four of five scientists surviving in the Celarium cocoon and the most junior. He willing acquiesced to his elder's unspoken command, moving sideways to the secondary unit. "There is flooding outside?" he asked.

"No." Makin shook his head, outwardly calm but inwardly seething with irritability. He must not allow his personal emotions to conflict with his duty. "The polar snows are turning to steam. I suspect this has also happened to the oceans." He shook his head a second time. "We have direct contact with the target?"

Sandric nodded his helmeted head with its attached conglomerate of instrumentation connecting him to the console by a twisting mass of wires and shimmering tubes.

"As Lexus stated," he reminded tensely, "and according to Pulse Responses, he – it – is in the receptive position."

Makin stared at the console. His lips twisted, his forehead puckered into a patchwork of worry lines, and his thoughts were troubled.

More than two lifetimes electronically probing a million solar systems, searching for a form of life that matched their own, and finally, we have located a small planet third from its own young sun. It was in a galaxy so far away the light from our exploding sun will not reach it until after that distant world's sun is also extinguished.

So far away—but the only planet that supported a human lifeform closely related to their own.

Yet, they are five hundred years behind in technological advancement.

Of course, they probably considered themselves advanced. The Orbitor Probe had detected man-made satellites circling their small world, and they appeared to have mastered visual communications. The Orbitor Pulse registered a high degree of mental intelligence in most of the planet's human population, although it varied between individuals.

Through the Orbitor Pulse they were able to connect with and measure the intellect of randomly selected individuals. This was a critical phase; mental capacity determined the ability of the individual not only to absorb, analyze, and use so much knowledge, but it needed to survive the impact impounded into the brain in a single power-pulse.

Finding a surrogate civilization was the primary mission in our fathers' time, when it was obvious our sun would become the holocaust destroying not only our planet but our entire solar system. Man would not, could not, survive the impending destruction. There was no escape from this planet or our star system.

In a scientific past almost beyond memory, the impossibility of space travel was proven. The human body could not survive prolonged periods of weightlessness, even in a state of suspended animation. The distance to any planet that might support life was beyond comprehension.

Now we are the old men, and it had been decreed, the accumulated scientific knowledge of our race must not die. Somehow, we must transfer it to another world and another race of people, so it would not only survive, but grow as knowledge should grow.

The implantation to a receptive human brain was not a problem. Generations earlier they realized the human brain was a physical computer receptive to correctly programmed input.

At first, implantation was a cumbersome and even painful process with the recipient encapsulated for several days. Success was not always achieved. It had become a simple and painless electronic process.

The Inflext Seeding took place in a designated laboratory, and it was essential the recipient remained rested until the seeding was complete.

An impossible mission, Makin thought, staring at the Orbitor Screen. That had been their first impression. Not only did they have to find a way of transferring the Inflext Seeding through an infinity of space, they had to locate a race of people equal to themselves, mentally if not physically.

Zarc, a famous scientist of the yesteryear, had determined life could only evolve relative to the output energy of the primary sun, the distance of the host planet from that sun, and the chemical and pressure components of its atmosphere. If nothing else, research had proven his theoretical equation correct.

Development of the Orbitor Pulse continued to astound as they discovered and extended the means to immediately analyze the mental capacity of any detected lifeform, no matter how distant. It could also be used, Zarc determined, to implant a single but complete Inflext Seeding across the same distance, if the detected lifeform satisfied the predetermined criteria.

However, the Pulse, which provided immediate feedback, revealed in every case where life was detected, physical intellect had not developed beyond the Primordial state. It was much too primitive for their purpose.

The search for a satisfactory surrogate dragged on, until it seemed no compatible life existed. There was frustration and anger, even hopelessness, as the torrid, reaching fingers of their malignant exploding sun scorched into the atmosphere and their world smoldered.

Then they located a tiny planet, so far away that the entire galaxy to which it belonged was little more than a smudge on the Orbital Scanner.

The Pulse Probe responded positively. Analysis was slow, demanding but promising. Life on the distant planet equated with theirs, although several hundred years behind in intellect. They were a scientific race, however, expanding rapidly in their knowledge and development. They appeared somewhat erratic in their behavior, registering mood swings and emotions that puzzled.

Were they of mind and matter sufficient to receive the greater knowledge of the dying world? Perhaps they had to be, Makin thought grimly. By all appearances, they were the only other intelligent human life form in the entire universe!

Doubt festered and grew as the Pulse Probe sought out and connected with one intellect after the other on that tiny world and rejected each as unsatisfactory. The Inflext Seeding criteria was demanding; it had to be. If the mental capacity was not of sufficient strength to receive the seeding, it could turn the brain to dust, resulting in madness and death.

Delusion replaced hope, despair became acute. As the days ticked by, hopelessness strained each of the scientists' countenances, over-shadowing even the sleeplessness in their eyes and the weariness in their faces.

Suddenly, the Pulse located an intellect that responded in parallel with the probing analysis, each segment of mental stimulus matching with the appropriate criterion. The symbolic positives flooded the screens of the receiving monitors.

Makin had demanded they test and re-test, despite frequent reminders from Lexus that time was running out. The inside walls of the Celarium were beginning to blister from the increasing outside heat.

He refused to be rushed; he had to be sure. The Factor of Acceptance had to be at the maximum. Any less and the receiving intellect would be destroyed. He did not, he believed, have that right. Too, there would be no second attempt. There would not be time.

The analytical positives continued. There were no negatives. The intellect to which the probe had attached itself was of the highest possible order, and very capable, according to the Probe, of not only receiving the Inflext Seeding, but of understanding and using the knowledge. The last, if not the least of the criteria, appeared to be a positive.

The Inflext Seeding, though it needed a wakeful brain for the initial input, induced a heavy trance-like "sleep" immediately afterwards, separating the brain from the body while the seeding took effect.

There appeared to be a rotation of seven periods in the existence of the Probe's connected lifeform, each period interspersed by a time of sleep. During six of the periods, the intellect was fiercely active, but each seventh period, there was a long spell of inaction. The intellect was awake yet completely at ease. Some type of rejuvenating period, Lexus determined, while the body recuperated and the brain rested—an ideal situation for the Inflext Seeding.

Makin was afraid to hope.

The recipient has to be at ease—not asleep—for the sleeping brain would not accept an Inflext transplant, but relaxed and without interference from any level of mental activity or anguish. There also needs to be a period afterwards, where the recipient will remain undisturbed.

The recipient was in a period of relaxation now, the probe set, and the Inflext Seeding primed to implant.

Is this distant intellect really the most suitable target? If only we could see what he—it—looks like. Makin's thoughts churned bitterly, doubts lingering. *All we know is its mental capacity, its ability to think and analyze and create. We know not its appearance, and the irrationality recorded in the responses from earlier connections is a peripheral concern. How do we know it will put the knowledge to proper use? Will it even know how to use it? If only there was vision as well as intellect—*

"Makin!" Lexus spoke urgently, disturbing his thoughts. "Look, to the wall..."

Cracks appeared between the blisters, and the blisters themselves were undulating.

Like the ocean waves, Makin thought irrationally. *But the oceans were no longer—they had turned to steam.*

"Our time is almost gone," Lexus continued grimly. "We must do it now!"

Four pairs of eyes watched as Makin stared at the screens, then wearily rubbed his hand across his face.

"Do it!" he snapped and wondered why he felt suddenly cold when it was growing so hot within the Celarium.

Sandric's helmeted head bent low over the console panel, and his fingers danced over the touch screen. Colored lights flickered across the Orbitor Screen and were replaced by a constant and rapid scrolling of symbols and numbers. A soft almost inaudible hum emitted from the upper part of Sandric's helmet, and the tubes connecting him to the console appeared to writhe with life.

Quickly, it was finished, and the screen spluttered and faded to a distant whirling of tiny flickering lights receding rapidly until they became nothing.

The screen faded to a final blackness.

No one moved or spoke until Lexus sat up, as though coming out of a trance, and began to remove his helmet.

"It is done," he murmured. "The Inflext Transplant was successful. The mental capacity of the receiving intellect has accepted it, and the programming is taking effect."

"The host rests undisturbed?" Makin asked.

"As the Pulse Probe indicated, his place of rest or rejuvenation is private. There is no other intellect within Probal range, and no reason to be concerned now that he is in a programming trance." Lexus nodded. "It is well, Makin. It is done. We are finished."

"We are finished," Makin agreed quietly and removed from the pocket of his tunic the small box containing five small pink pills...

———————

"I don't understand," Mary Quinn said, angrily wiping tears from her eyes. "He went fishing alone below the headland every Sunday. His Peaceful Place, he

called it, away from all the worries and the stresses of his work. No one to disturb him, he said. It was His Special Place. He knew the sea, and he knew the tides. And it wasn't a heart attack or drugs—nothing like that, they said.

"It was almost as if he was asleep—but how could a man not wake when the water reached him? How could a man sleep while the tide rose up and drowned him....?"

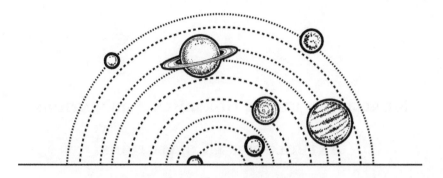

About the Editor

Devora Gray is the creator and host of "Dear Sweet and Low: Relationship Advice for Busy People." She is the author of *Tell the Wolves I'm Home: An Erotic Werewolf Origin Story Human Furniture and the Quest for the Perfect Woman*. Under the nonfiction pen name D.A. Langley, she blogs about life, kink, travel, and philosophy, but has a disclaimer. "I don't know which I love more: writing my own stories or editing others." When not rolling in a large pile of books, she enjoys CrossFit, hiking, and cosplay with her partner in Las Vegas, NV. You can find her on Facebook, Instagram, TikTok, and Medium.com (writing as D.A. Langley).

More books from 4 Horsemen Publications

Anthologies & Collections

4HP Anthologies
Teen Angst: Mix Vol. 1
Teen Angst: Mix Vol. 2
My Wedding Date
The Offices of Supernatural Being
The Sentient Space

Demonic Anthologies
Demonic Wildlife
Demonic Household
Demonic Carnival
Demonic Classics
Demonic Vacations
Demonic Medicine
Demonic Workplace
& more to follow!

Fantasy, SciFi, & Paranormal Romance

Beau Lake
The Beast Beside Me
The Beast Within Me
Taming the Beast: Novella
The Beast After Me
Charming the Beast: Novella
The Beast Like Me
An Eye for Emeralds
Swimming in Sapphires
Pining for Pearls

Danielle Orsino
Locked Out of Heaven
Thine Eyes of Mercy

From the Ashes
Kingdom Come
Fire, Ice, Acid, & Heart

J.M. Paquette
Klauden's Ring
Solyn's Body
The Inbetween
Hannah's Heart
Call Me Forth
Invite Me In
Keep Me Close

DISCOVER MORE AT
4HORSEMENPUBLICATIONS.COM

CPSIA information can be obtained
at www.ICGtesting.com
Printed in the USA
BVHW071825240123
656981BV00005B/868

9 798823 200059